Only the Lonely

Also by **THE AUTHOR**

Someone You Know

Only the Lonely
A Novel

Gary Zebrun

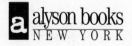
alyson books
NEW YORK

Manufactured in the
United States of America

A trade paperback original published by Alyson Books
245 West 17th Street, New York, NY 10011

Distribution in the United Kingdom by Turnaround Publisher Services Ltd.
Unit 3, Olympia Trading Estate, Coburg Road, Wood Green
London N22 6TZ England

First Edition: September 2008

08 09 10 11 12 13 14 15 16 17 a 10 9 8 7 6 5 4 3 2 1

ISBN-10: 1-5-9350-084-X
ISBN-13: 978-1-59350-084-9

Library of Congress Cataloging-in-Publication data are on file.

Cover design by Victor Mingovits

For Edmund White

How do things end, finally, things such as this—peter out
to some forgotten core of weary faithful huddled in the rain?
—Don DeLillo, *Underworld*

Tuesday, September 4, 2001
LITTLE GREEN BIRDS

T HE BOX WAS WRAPPED in a *Buffalo News* comics page. Asim didn't hear his brother leave it outside the office at the Bethlehem Theater because he had been lost in the University of Michigan catalogue, studying a photograph of students sitting cross-legged on a campus quad, nearby a Calder sculpture—a huge red rudder—rising into the air. Stuck into the ground was a little rainbow flag. One of the guys looked Arab, maybe Iranian, he couldn't tell. There was a blond girl, probably with Polish parents; a freckled, dopey-looking Irish kid; a handsome guy, maybe nineteen, with thick black hair, no doubt Italian. They were laughing. He thought, *they must be gay.*

Inside the theater, *Shrek* was playing for the last time; he could hear Rufus Wainwright singing "Hallelujah" while Shrek and the Donkey ambled to Town Square. Asim knew he didn't have a good voice like Sonia and Billy. He couldn't sing like his father. But he hummed along, listening for the lyrics: *It's not a cry you can hear at night / It's not somebody who's seen the light / It's a cold and it's a broken hallelujah.*

Asim tossed the catalogue onto the desk, and wondered, *how stupid am I, staying here.* He looked at his watch: it was past the time he should have made an aisle walk. He'd forgotten to check on Sonia, who had been too tired to see the movie on opening night; he worried she might have drifted off in her seat.

On his way out, he tripped over the box. He poked around the lobby and went outside to the sidewalk. Across the street a white van with a Bubble Brush Car Wash sign pulled away and sped off. He believed he'd recognized the driver. *Shit*, he thought, *was that Tarik? Can he be back?*

He took the box into the office. Taped to it was an envelope, and inside a cassette—no note—though he recognized his brother's handwriting on the label: *For Asim. Paradise? Or Hell?* Above the inscription Tarik had drawn little green birds flying in a purple sky.

He placed the tape into a portable Sony and listened:

"I am swimming in all of Allah's expectation. There are other ways to *jihad*, but this one is sweetest. The desert taught me about sacrifice, which Mother understood. I don't know why Father called her Sinai crazy. If she knew about me, she would shout out, 'Praise Allah, who granted me honor with my *Shahid*.' Sometimes I think about you as a boy, not a dirty faggot, and I wonder, *If only I could help Asim.* I had to fight off Father's demons, too."

After a scraping silence, Asim thought the tape had finished, and just as he reached to click off the player, his brother's voice returned: "Why is that Russian bitch living at our house? I've got to see you. You should have delivered the imam's package. He had plans for you at Michigan. Now I think he believes that I can't be trusted with a brother like you. He'll see. Inside the box is a Jew's skull. The ashes are from an Afghan *shisha*. It is an inspiration."

He unwrapped the newspaper—Doonesbury, Zippy, Garfield, Rose is Rose—and opened the lid. The skull was about the size of a small cantaloupe. Its top was sawed off, and he could see the ashes in the cavity.

He lifted the thing from the box and cringed. He thought, *he's fucking crazier than I knew.*

"What's that?" Sonia asked, from the doorway.

"A globe for a lamp in the lobby," he said, rushing to replace the lid. He opened the bottom cabinet drawer and put it in. He remembered the tape and popped it out of the player, and dropped it in, too. When he closed the door, he caught his finger.

"I thought I heard a voice. It sounded a little like Tarik," she said.

"You're hearing things again."

She grimaced.

"You look sick," she said.

He ignored her and asked, "Did you like *Shrek*?"

"Who wouldn't," she said.

February 2001
OPENING NIGHT

ASIM KNEW OTHERS in Lackawanna called her crazy because she spoke Russian and wavered when she walked. When he saw her again at the Bethlehem Theater after his father died, he understood Sonia was sick with the shaking disease. It was the last show of *Notting Hill*; she handed him her ticket, and he felt her fingers skittering across his palm.

"They call Hugh Grant another Cary. *Nyet*. You're as beautiful as the boy in that launderette movie," she said.

"Omar," Asim said.

"Who?"

"That's the boy's name."

There were only fourteen moviegoers in the theater. While *Not-*

ting Hill played, he walked down the aisle a couple of times, pretending he needed something from the storage room behind the screen. He wanted to check her out, and each time he walked back, he'd catch a glimpse; with a prurient interest that surprised him, he thought, *She's the woman my father loved.*

He was five when he first saw them. The door to the room next to the projection booth was cracked open. His father tumbled, naked, with Sonia on a cot the size of a bunk bed. The old man lifted himself and fell back. He breathed like the warty-faced Czech with asthma who lived next door. Asim watched until his father rose from the cot, blocking Sonia from his view. The old man stepped into boxers and pulled on his trousers and then, still bare-chested, turned and noticed his son. Asim bolted down to the theater and hid under a seat until the houselights went on, and the old man found him scrunched there like he'd been the one who'd done something wrong. (His father liked to be called *old man* because it made him think of Ernest Hemingway and bullfights and the sea.)

"Since when did you become a detective?" his old man asked, sitting next to him and patting his head.

"Our secret," his father said.

A couple of years before Asim's father died, the old man had watched him set down a canister of film outside the room with the cot. On the door was a *Sabrina* poster that his father had hung there years before: Audrey Hepburn arm and arm with Humphrey Bogart and William Holden. The old man seemed washed in regret. He looked back at his son and opened the door and sat on the cot.

"Be kind to her when you take over the movie house. You'll understand. Love isn't easy."

"Kind to who?"

"Sonia."

"What makes you think I want to stay around, Dad?"

"You love the movies. It's a family business. You can make a good life in Lackawanna. Anyway, she's going to need some company."

"You aren't enough *company.*"

"Don't be a smart-ass."

"Why would she need me? You don't look like you're going anywhere."

The old man didn't say anything, as if he wasn't listening anymore, and Asim decided he'd try to rattle his father.

"So what was playing when I found you fucking her?"

It was the first time he mentioned what he had seen in the cot room.

"How should I remember? That's a stupid thing to ask."

"Almost as stupid as thinking I'm going to live and die in Lackawanna."

"Go off somewhere and see if you'll ever be as happy as you could be at the Bethlehem. You'll come home. You'll see."

The first time she came back to the theater, Asim's father had been dead for two months. Asim stopped at the top of the aisle and noticed Sonia laughing in her seat. He tried to turn his attention to Hugh Grant and Julia Roberts, but all he could think about was his father pulling up boxer shorts in the room upstairs. Since that night when he was five, to his surprise he sometimes spied on the old man when his father dressed at home. Even a few months ago, he had been watching from the open door of his bedroom. Tarik noticed. Their father wasn't shy about nakedness, and Asim was thinking, *He still has legs like a younger man's.*

His brother shouted, "Close your door. It offends Allah to show off your body like this."

His father yelled, "We aren't in Egypt. Don't tell me what to do." He patted his bare chest like a gorilla and smiled.

Tarik glared at the old man and walked into Asim's room and said, "I don't know why Allah allows him to live." His brother slammed the door. Not long ago, Tarik had warned him, "Like father, like son. Watch out."

Notting Hill was in its last reel. Asim thought, *The old man must have known I liked boys. He should have talked to me about it.*

Asim still had to restock the candy shelves. The keys hung in the office from the side of the desk in a narrow space next to the wall. When he sat to reach for them, a tear in the vinyl cushion pricked his thigh, and he decided to fix it before the slit got worse. He opened a drawer where his father had kept tools and duct tape. On top of everything was an airline ticket for his brother to Islamabad. It was dated April 5 and didn't have a return. He wondered why his brother would want to go to Pakistan but wasn't surprised Tarik hadn't told anyone. Except for outbursts and mumbling in Arabic, his brother seldom said much to anyone. He could understand a trip to Egypt to see their mother, though Asim himself had decided he didn't want to go there, ever; or a flight to Jordan where his uncles Usef and Salum lived, but Islamabad didn't make any sense.

He couldn't think of anyone Tarik would even walk around the block to see. He searched through drawers for anything else his brother might have left in the desk that would explain what was going on, but there were just movie house things: copies of *Variety*, concession and advertising invoices, spools of colored tickets, old movie stills. He held up John Travolta in *Saturday Night Fever* and thought, *he's hot.* Those Aussies in *Strictly Ballroom.* Gene Kelly swinging around a lamppost in *Singin' in the Rain.* He wondered whether his father ever danced with the Russian woman. He rolled up the Travolta to take it home. He decided he would talk to Masika first and see what she thought about the ticket. But he already knew what she would say: "Don't worry about our crazy brother. Let him go and disappear in the desert."

He found the tape and patched the slit in the cushion.

After everyone had left, he chained shut the emergency doors. On his way out he was surprised to find her standing in the lobby next to the coming attractions—Pierce Brosnan bungee-jumping out of a window to retrieve a suitcase full of money in *The World Is Not Enough.* Sonia was smoking a cigarette with a silver plastic holder, threads of smoke iridescent in the chandelier light.

"Where's the usher?" she asked.

She was confused. Her eyes wandered to the lobby cards and some old stills—Chaplin, Davis, Dean, Monroe—suspended from the ceiling, until she settled on his dark eyes and waited for an answer.

"What usher?" Asim asked.

Sonia bowed her head, and he worried that she was going to start bawling.

"I knew Joseph for a long time. Before him there was Andrew, and before him, a few ushers I never thought to ask their names. I was young. I didn't shake."

"I'm sorry," he said.

"Who are you?"

He didn't know if she was asking his name or if it was the question of an old woman lost in her past.

"Asim," he said.

He could tell she was thinking about the name, and then she said, "An old name for a boy."

He shrugged.

"You're Badru's youngest. You've never worked here."

"I've been here almost all day, every Saturday since I was a little kid."

"I know."

"You do?"

"Your father was a gentleman."

He nodded.

"Sometimes he'd bring popcorn to my seat."

He didn't say anything, and wondered whether she knew he'd seen them all those years ago.

"Your brother isn't so gentle."

"You know Tarik?"

"He sulks."

"How do you know so much about everyone?"

"Your sister's beautiful. A nurse."

"You're a little creepy."

She smiled. "I like you."

What could he say?

"Sometimes your father couldn't get away, and he asked the usher to drive me home. We sat in the car and talked about the movie," she said.

"I'll take you tonight. I know stuff about you, too." He was surprised by how much he liked her.

"A celebrity," she said.

"It's been two months since my father died. Where have you been? I thought you came to all the openers."

"Don't talk about the dead."

She put her hand, which had begun to tremble more erratically, on his arm and followed him out the last open glass door. The movie house keys jingled from a brass ring as he locked it. She shuffled beside him to the car, parked across Abbott Road outside the Pig Iron, a men's bar, Poles and Irish stinking of their joblessness and drinking their last boilermakers of the night. Through the window he noticed a guy in a tank top, with a shock of red disheveled hair, watching him open the door of his beat-up El Dorado, a gift from an uncle who owned convenience stores in Buffalo. He thought, *A tank top in February. That's something.* He helped the old woman into the front seat. When he closed the door and looked back, he saw a few others at the window, but only the redhead was watching. The guy was older and Asim had noticed him hanging out in the park by the lake. Asim didn't turn to see but hoped, by the time he drove away, the redhead would still be watching.

"Where do you live, Sonia?" he asked.

Sonia— it was a name that made him think of a black dress with diamonds and fur. It sounded like drag.

"Across the DB Mart," she said.

"On Wilkesbarre?"

She nodded.

"I've never seen you in the neighborhood," he said.

"I've seen you." She was staring at him.

Asim wanted to ask where, but instead he remembered what Tarik had said about her: *abomination*. It was what his brother said about their father. It was what Tarik said about fags.

"Okay," he paused, and said, "let's go."

He had figured she lived on the other side of the bridge, a neighborhood close to Our Lady of Victory, with other European immigrants whose sons and daughters built raised ranches with automatic garage doors, plastic on couches, jockeys or Marys-on-the-half-shells dotting lawns. Why would she live in Arab town?

"There," she said, pointing to a triple-decker with a busted porch globe, the bulb, exposed, dangling.

"Are you a Communist?" she asked.

He shook his head and smiled awkwardly because the question was ridiculous.

"Don't worry. Nicholas believed he was a Communist."

"Who's Nicholas?"

"My husband. Your father liked him. Too much."

"*Too much*. What's that supposed to mean?"

She opened her door and leaned back into the car and said, "*Razrishiti vam pamoch.*"

"What's that?" he asked. "You aren't making any sense."

"Someday you'll know," she said, and turned.

Asim watched her climb the porch steps and enter the door into the house. He waited until he saw a third-floor light illuminate a window. He wondered whether she'd look out, but it wasn't long before the room darkened. He stayed a while looking for another light to pop on and pictured the *Sabrina* poster—Nicholas and his father arm and arm with Sonia. He realized what Sonia had meant by *too much*. But he suspected she made things up to seem mysterious. *Raz . . . vam . . . mook, whatever,* he thought. Could the Russian words have had something to do with his father loving Sonia's husband? If his father had liked men too, wouldn't the old man have said something to Asim? Again he thought about what Tarik had said, *abomination*. It made him shiver. When no other lights came on, he drove a few blocks down Wilkesbarre to the house he'd lived in all of his life. Along the way, he thought, *My father must have been nuts to think I'd stay in Lackawanna for her, or anyone.*

BLACK-AND-WHITE

LONG BEFORE COLOR, Sonia and her mother hid out at the Bethlehem Theater and watched black-and-white icons flicker through the hole in the projection booth. Later, when they were home alone, they listened to the radio whine with light-and-dark sensations from voices of singers with bewildering names like Billie Holiday, Bing Crosby, and The Duke. Sometimes she watched her mother write, black-and-white words, like the images they saw at the movies. The old woman was retrieving memories and had to write carefully because her crippled hands trembled like twigs.

Now years later, there were evenings when Sonia, her own

hands shaking, would sit before her kitchen window for hours and imagine smoke curling from the stacks of the abandoned Bethlehem Steel mill, and picture herself in a Russian forest where her fingers in another life might have actually been twigs upon a creaking body, wooden and rooted to the earth. Or she saw herself as Saint Sophia in the folktale of Glemkin Woods, hiding out underneath the roots of a huge birch. She had never been to Russia, but she loved her mother's stories about the dead returning every springtime: one came back a bear, another an owl, still another a spider or a snake.

Lackawanna itself was cast in light and dark as if it were the backdrop for all the shadowy movies ever made about America. Movies where a beautiful woman was thrown, beaten and dying, out of a car into an alleyway, her diamond-studded brooch, wondrous and accusing, beaming in the darkness. She loved the black-and-white films as much as she loved the Russian forest. She remembered a scene from a movie she couldn't name anymore: Richard Widmark struck down a girl on a street much like any street in Lackawanna. It was night. The fog was oceanic. Clutching her arms, Widmark called her a two-timing dame.

"You belong in the gutter," he said, "with the rest of the city's trash."

He hit her hard across the face. Her eyes were lit in the sprawl of a floodlight, where the girl had fallen back in a filthy corner. Years ago, when she saw this scene at the Bethlehem, she imagined her mother was that woman. Controlled and accusing, her mother stared at Widmark, while nearby someone played something that sounded like Louis Armstrong's low, uncompromising horn. The foggy glow of the lamplight shone all the while on her as she watched Widmark walk away.

Back from seeing *Notting Hill*, in the darkness of her apartment, with movies jumbled in her head, Sonia looked outside her bedroom window to the street lit by the neon light of the DB Mart. *The store is run by Arabs*, she thought. *Years ago markets had real names: Lapinski's, Gallagher's, Caruso's.* Next to it was the soccer field where the Arab boys played. It was there she used to watch Asim and think, *He should have been my son.* But now it was night and all she could see was the store's neon splashing red on the asphalt. She imagined herself in the street, which was a little like the Widmark movie, or a London street in the Hugh Grant movie, or the starry blackness inside a Russian forest. She couldn't tell where she was. She didn't care. She didn't care if all around her night prowlers passed all night long, because she disappeared when the neon light flashed on and emerged again when it blinked back off. She didn't care if boys called her crazy. Boys had called her mother crazy, too. The past stayed as close to her as the light her mother described lingering over the forest during melancholy white nights in Russia, those unbridled northern days in summer when almost nothing, it seemed, would die. She saw the boy's Cadillac drive away.

"Asim," she said, just to hear the name. Now he'd finally spoken to her. She thought his dark eyes were as inscrutable as Nicholas's.

She remembered the night her father brought Nicholas home. He was taking off his boots in the foyer when she came downstairs. She was seventeen. Even now she remembered her excitement as she watched the arc of his back that night. Outside it had been snowing for hours, furious squalls that sometimes blow across Lake Erie south of Buffalo in late autumn, before the water freezes and the heavy wet snow piles up four, even five inches every hour. When he rose from his half-moon curl and she saw his dark eyes, she knew she wanted him.

"Say 'hi' to Nicky," her father said.

He lived in South Buffalo and worked in the Lackawanna steel mill with her father. His hair was black and thick and shiny. His nose slightly Roman and the shadow on his face swarthy and mysterious. Even then she saw his restlessness. She remembered his surprised smile when he noticed her; she remembered a draft from the door that made her shiver. Or at least at the time she thought it had been the draft, and not just the sight of him.

"I said, say 'hi' to our new *goombah*. I told him tonight he's eating borscht and pigs' feet."

Her mother walked into the hallway, and her father glared at his wife in the way that terrified Sonia. She hoped he wouldn't strike her mother, not with the new boy in the house. Nicholas looked at her with those eyes that reflected more than they revealed and she sheltered herself inside them. Later that night, when she was in bed and Nicholas was asleep on the couch downstairs and the wind-driven snow was hitting her window, she imagined lying beside him. At first she was afraid when minutes later he appeared in the room and slipped off his sooty T-shirt and boxer shorts. He climbed into bed and slid one of his large hands under her head and raised himself just enough to lean in and kiss her. She had dreamed of a boy like him for so long, someone who wouldn't hit her. Her lover would be olive-skinned. He'd be tender. He'd want to take care of her, and when they were together no one else would matter.

That night, after they had made love, he told her that he wanted everything from his life and, if they ended up together, she'd help him write speeches about fair wages and shorter workdays, safety in the mill. He said her father had told him she wanted to go to Buffalo State and be a teacher and a writer. He rose from the bed and slipped on his boxer shorts, red, she remembered, Marxist red, and carried his T-shirt in his hand. He had been quiet and gentle, careful not to wake anyone. He leaned over and kissed her. His restlessness had vanished. There was no hint of the disappointments that would consume him. Before he left, he said he'd fetch her Friday night and take her to see *Born Yesterday* at the Bethlehem. She remembered clearly, he used the word "fetch" and how it made her happy. And then she was filled with worry because she remembered he had said earlier, "if they ended up together." Even then she was impatient with qualifiers. For a long time she couldn't sleep, and in the morning, Nicholas Salvaggio and her father were gone before she woke.

Asim, she thought, *he could be a Communist. He's Nicholas in an Arab skin. He's prettier than Badru. I used to tell his father, "I wish I had a son." And now, poor boy, his father's dead. I could be a better mother than the Sinai crazy. He needs someone to care about him. He needs me. Who cares if he's already a man? If I were younger, I could be his lover.*

YOU CAN HAVE ALLAH

ASIM LIVED AT 108 Wilkesbarre Avenue, five blocks from the Yemen Soccer Field. From his bedroom window he could see the onion dome of the Lackawanna Guidance Mosque, which used to be the Ukrainian Orthodox Church. As far as he knew his father never answered a single *adhan*. But for about a year Tarik had followed the call to daily prayer and tried to convince Asim to attend. "Get lost," he finally told his brother. "I'm like Dad. You can have Allah."

Tarik had nearly decked him.

When he got home, Asim was surprised his brother was listening to television in the bedroom. He could hear laughter from an audience and David Letterman introducing a dog that could bark along to "Take Me Out to the Ball Game." Tarik must have fallen asleep during the 11 o'clock news. For a moment he thought about barging in and asking about the ticket to Pakistan, but it was late and he knew a question like this could set off his brother. The neighbor might call the police again. He'd wait. Across the hall a light shone under the door of his sister's room. She liked to read for hours after a night at the hospital. He knocked.

"Asim," she said.

He walked in. "Who else would it be?"

"How was Julia Roberts?"

He ignored her.

"Something's wrong," she said.

He took the ticket out of his pocket and said, "I found this in the office desk. It's a plane ticket for Tarik to Pakistan."

"You're kidding, right? Wishful thinking?"

"No, look."

She was sitting up in the bed, a *Vogue* magazine opened to a spread about Ewan McGregor in *Moulin Rouge* on her lap. She took the ticket.

"That's weird. Who does he know in Islamabad?"

"That's what I wondered."

"He's probably off to some religious thing." She thought for a few seconds and said, "Some pilgrimage, you know, like to Mecca."

"Mecca's in Saudi Arabia."

"I know, stupid. I bet it's something to do with the mosque. Anyway, who cares, *really*. Good riddance, for a while."

"Maybe I should say something."

He was surprised she wasn't worried.

"He should have gone to Egypt with Mother," she said, looking back at her magazine. "Check out Ewan McGregor. We should get this movie."

"I guess," he said, quickly losing interest because he couldn't get Tarik out of his head.

"He's good-looking, isn't he?" she said, teasing Asim.

He gave her a look, and left.

He thought of going back in and telling her he had seen Sonia. But he decided he'd wait until the morning.

The three Zahids had lived by themselves since their father was killed on Ridge Road. He was stopped at the light not far from the theater when Joey Phalen, driving a pickup on the way to the Pig Iron, plowed into him. Asim had been changing the marquee and saw everything. He ran to the scene. Joey, who used to coach him on the Pee Wee Bandits, was drunk. By the time Asim got there, Joey was out of the pickup looking for damage and mumbling, "Fuck me, fuck me, what the fuck did I do now," while inside his car, Asim's father slumped over the steering wheel. The medical examiner said Badru's heart had given out and maybe the shock of the impact contributed, but the doctor wasn't sure.

A few weeks after the old man was buried, Asim's mother, Salama, prepared to leave for her home in Egypt. It was late December and it still hadn't snowed. Lake fog skulked across the backyard when she appeared draped in Muslim clothes, from head to foot, that he had never seen her wear before. His father detested the *hijab* and had forbidden it. Asim remembered him saying, "Why are Muslim men so afraid their women will be molested? A woman shouldn't hide her beauty." But the day she left, free now to do whatever she wished, his mother—only her face and hands visible—seemed even more a stranger than she'd always been to him. She said she had tried to love them in her way. "You are Americans," she said, looking at Asim and then Masika. "You are your father's children. I'm tired of America." She told them that someday she hoped they would see the yellow desert stretching through temples and scrub, the place where she wanted to die, far from Lackawanna. Then, they would understand. She turned to Tarik and said, "Take me to the airport."

Tarik had stood beside her silently; Asim was too surprised to react. Masika, though, had grown angry, and shouted, "Go to your stupid desert and burn. This is how you honor our dead father."

Asim reached out to his mother and said, "Don't listen to her. Stay."

Tarik slapped Masika across the face.

Asim grabbed his brother, and shouted, "No!"

Tarik started to fight, but their mother held him back and demanded, "Enough, take me away." At the sound of her voice, he wilted. Hours later, when he returned, he walked past his brother and sister and murmured, "Allah plots against unbelievers."

"He's lost," Masika said.

"Maybe without her, he'll—"

She interrupted him and said, "Nothing good is ever going to come from today."

Weeks later the three returned to the theater, which had been shut since their father died. It was January. They were surprised when Tarik joined them. On a lobby door was this sign: OKAY, TOWELHEADS, OPEN UP THE SHOW.

Tarik tore it down and said, "Fuck them."

Inside the office, Tarik removed a photo from the wall—their father standing with Sonia and Nicholas in the lobby—and hurled it against the desktop.

"Fuck him. We should sell this hellhole, but keep it if you want. You're cut from the same cloth as our stupid father," he said.

"What's that supposed to mean?" Asim asked.

Their brother paused, and said, "They should shoot you all."

"Tarik." Asim was incredulous.

"Bastard," Masika said.

Asim worried she was about to strike him, but Tarik walked off without another word. Asim thought, *They, who's they?*

He fished the photo from the shattered frame and swept up the broken glass with a piece of cardboard. He wondered whether he shouldn't give the theater a shot. Tarik didn't want anything to do with it. His sister was too busy at the hospital. Maybe his father was right. Maybe he could be happy at the Bethlehem. He figured he had six months before he was supposed to start at Michigan. It was worth a try. He thought about Sonia and wondered why she hadn't gone to his father's funeral. He remembered his old man saying: "I want you to get to know her. No one except the Russian loves movies as much as we do, son."

It was the first time he could remember his father calling him son.

"Why should I care about your lover?" he had asked, irritated.

"Don't be stupid. Don't talk about her if you can't be kind," the old man said.

Asim wondered why Sonia had picked tonight to return to the Bethlehem for the first time since his father's death. It couldn't have been *Notting Hill*. He closed his bedroom door and undressed, but before going to sleep he fished out the photo of his father with Sonia and Nicholas that he'd stuffed into his sock drawer. He propped it up against the edge of his computer screen and clicked on Google. He typed in the word *razrishiti*. He'd tried to remember what Sonia had said in the car and hoped the first word was close enough to get a hit. Nothing. Not even a *Do you mean . . . ?* He clicked off.

In bed, he thought, *I'm glad I finally talked to her and she thinks I look like Omar.* Before falling asleep, he remembered the scene from *My Beautiful Laundrette,* in which Johnny and Omar walk into the launderette's back room and undress behind the glass where no one can see in, as if they're in a love story playing to an empty movie house. He remembered the John Travolta still and got up and taped it to the wall beside his computer. "I could have been a contend-ah," he whispered, mixing movie heroes. He thought of the *Sabrina* poster and tried to picture Nicholas, probably olive-skinned like John Travolta, naked beside his father, even darker, *handsome for an Arabian,* Lackawanna women used to say. He was surprised when he discovered his cock was hard.

THE WORLD IS NOT ENOUGH

SONIA BOARDED THE BUS on Wilkesbarre for the five-minute ride to the Bethlehem. It was 8:45, the last run of the night. When she passed the basilica, she thought of a dream her grandmother had told her mother in Russia: *Votive candles are burning in a cave before the solitary icon of the Mother of God. The cave is crowded with the faces of men and women that have fallen onto the hard black dirt. All around is the sound of sighing. Soon the face of the Mother of God falls into the other faces, and all of them begin to wail because Our Lady of Tenderness is lost among them. The candles burn out. In the dark cave the faces wail.*

She was seven when her mother told her this dream, and afterward her mother said, "Your grandmother could be a trouble-maker; she liked to tell me scary things. It's better for us here, in America."

That was the end of summer 1939. The next morning her mother had an ear to the radio, listening to a reporter say Adolf Hitler had invaded Poland. She asked, "What does 'invaded' mean?" Her mother ignored her. Sonia left and walked to the lakeshore near Father Nelson Baker's Home for Boys. She collected stones and washed them clean in the water. She named them: round red jewel, white-specked pearl, clipped angel wing, devil's paw. Nearby she discovered a dead blackbird, its talons slack like the collapsed legs of a huge spider. A priest from the home appeared. He was wearing a chocolate robe down to his ankles, sandals that barely contained fat, misshapen toes with thick nails burnt gray like lichen-covered stones bulging from the earth. His face was un-shaven, and when he smiled, his mouth was a red wound. Sonia bolted for home. When she told her mother about the dead bird and the priest at the shore, her mother embraced her and said, "Why worry about a dead bird and a priest?"

Later that night she could hear the radio downstairs: her mother singing something about a blackbird and a radio voice talking about Hitler again. Her father had walked in, drunk, and she heard him screaming about the war in the old country and couldn't under-stand what was going on, and then she heard the slap across her mother's face. She heard him climb the stairs and pass her room without pausing in the doorway as he would when he wasn't drunk. After he had closed his door, she heard something in the backyard and looked out and saw her mother sitting on a huge tree stump.

She opened the window and could hear her mother singing just loud enough that Sonia knew it was about the blackbird packing up its cares and woes. In the morning, they didn't talk about what had happened. They never did.

The bus stopped outside the Bethlehem and the driver had to call to her that she was there. She was halfway to the back. There were only four other passengers: two old men who were going to the Knights of Columbus Hall, a hairdresser named Dorothy probably on her way back from a shut-in, and a Middle Eastern man, maybe forty, more foreign than any of the Arabs in town. His eyes were fixed and disapproving. He wore a cotton hat the color of blood that stopped halfway down his forehead like a woven bucket. His beard was short and wiry. When she passed him, she smiled but he sat, stone-faced, watching her all the while. She thought, *He's thinking I look like some old, scarred whore.* Badru used to warn her about his type—serious, attracted to and repelled by everything sexy. It was the way Tarik watched her.

"You look good tonight, Sonia," Johnny, the driver, said.

She'd put on more makeup than usual, to please Asim. Her lipstick was strawberry red. She'd slid a small pearl comb into her silver hair, not white like so many other old women in town. Her bright red silk scarf had made her look Bohemian. *Young men like eccentric-looking older women,* she thought.

"It's opening night," she said.

"What's playing?"

"You pass here a dozen times a week and don't look at the marquee." She rapped her fingers on his shoulder and said, "Shame, Johnny. It's *The World Is Not Enough.* "

"I liked the old Bond better."

"Sean Connery."

"That's right."

"I like them all."

She stepped off the bus and waited for it to pull away before she crossed the street. As it did, she saw the stranger was watching her from the bus window.

Asim had seen her coming, and he went to the heavy glass lobby door to open it for her.

"I was waiting," he said. "The movie goes on any minute now. Place is crowded."

She took four one-dollar bills from her purse and handed them to him. She'd noticed his eagerness and was pleased because it felt almost like a kind of flirting.

"Senior ticket, please," she said.

There was no cashier, there never was anymore, so he went into the booth and punched out a ticket.

"The stub," she said.

"It's okay, I know you paid."

"I want the stub. I keep them. I started with a cigar box, then a shoe box, and now they're all stuffed into a dress box from Klien-hans."

He was worried that he had upset her. He tore off the stub and said, "I'm sorry."

"No harm. You can call me Sonia, dear."

All of a sudden the boy seemed uncomfortable, and Sonia, afraid she was trying too hard, said, "Don't worry. I call everyone '*dear*'."

It wasn't true.

She took the torn ticket and slipped it into her purse. She walked past, and her hand, unoccupied with her shiny black bag, trembled more furiously than when she'd arrived. He made sure she had found a seat before he darkened the house. She picked out her favorite spot, about halfway down the burgundy carpeted slope with big golden Bs for "Bethlehem" woven down the center. She slipped past a young couple at the aisle, glad she had made it before the movie started. Seconds before the lights went out, she thought: *There's something fundamentally tragic about the boy, like Nicky, like Badru.* She was troubled by the word "fundamentally" and wished it hadn't popped into her head. She was sorry she'd missed so many opening nights, but she hadn't believed she could bear the Bethlehem without Badru. She was wrong. Badru had left her Asim. *I'll make sure the kid gets a laugh or two,* she thought. Then came the moment of pitch blackness, a little like death, before the flickering light from the projection booth filled the screen with what she'd waited for all week.

GOOD LOVE GONE BAD

ASIM HAD SEEN THE early show and didn't like it: the opening credits when liquid shapes morphed into women like molten jell in a lava lamp, the stiff lady M, the stupid chase on the Thames in a boat that looked like some stealth bomber, which he didn't like either. He didn't like Elektra because he knew a woman in Azerbaijan could never own oil fields or lose a million dollars in a casino. He hated the stereotype of the bright, starry oil-driven future of the Western world. He hated Baku and Istanbul, Islamabad and Baghdad, Tel Aviv, and even his father's Cairo. He couldn't find half of these places on a globe. He hated endless desert sand. He hated Islam. He wished Palestine and Israel would vanish from the face of the earth. *Poosh*. He was glad his mother was gone. He wondered about the Irish and the Polish in Lackawanna. Did they resist so much of their parents' old worlds? He hated the city's soot. He didn't think he hated America. He liked its movies and soccer, shaking Sonia. He laughed. He liked American boys. *At Michigan,* he thought, *There'd be lots of boys.* Then Renard appeared on the screen: He was Bond's nemesis, a bullet in his skull withering his senses so that he felt nothing and grew stronger every day until he died. Renard was strangely handsome. He was angry like Tarik.

Asim wished he wasn't so weak. He wished he could stand up to Tarik. He wished he loved someone.

He restocked the concession stand, swept and mopped the lobby floor. He remembered that he had Tarik's plane ticket and returned it to the drawer in the office. He still hadn't asked his brother about it, and wondered whether his sister wasn't right: "Let him go. Who cares? Maybe he'll never come back." In a mocking voice, she'd said, "Free at last, free at last." He paused, leaned on the mop, more anxious than he'd been in a long time, and thought, *She doesn't really mean that.*

He replaced the coming attractions display that still had Bond bungee-jumping from a window with shots from next week's film, *Memento.* It was the last independent his father had ordered. The old man had believed that for every three blockbusters he was obligated to show a movie that he might love or that might make people think. "You lose a little money," he had told Asim. "But you feel a little like an artist."

Asim took a seat in the back and watched the last hour of 007 scurrying in the desert. Veiled women carrying baskets on their shoulders reminded him of his mother. He thought of the ceaseless times she had sat silent through dinner, her head bowed so that she didn't have to look at anyone. Days after the night he had found his father with Sonia, he was eating with the family and wanted to say, "I saw Father naked with someone." But he remembered what his father had told him—"our secret"—and instead he tapped his mother on the shoulder and said, "You don't look happy." He was five. In a rare instance of sympathy, she tried to force a smile, but even then he knew it wasn't what she had felt. He never knew what she felt. Tarik and Masika looked uncomfortable. His father shook his head. For days Asim repeatedly asked his father what was wrong with her, and the old man finally said, "She can't help herself. She's Sinai crazy." His old man told him God makes some people hopeless. Asim didn't ask what "hopeless" meant and didn't want to know what "Sinai crazy" was and wondered whether she had found out about Sonia and whether that had made her so silent. What saddened him as he grew older was that he understood what loveless lives they had shared. His father found solace with Sonia. His mother cherished dreams of the desert.

On the screen sandstone stretched across the landscape and he imagined his mother melting into shimmering yellow heat. He was relieved when Renard appeared, slipping his shirt over his head and revealing a chest that Asim wanted to touch. He looked over to find Sonia and noticed her head drifting to her shoulder; she quickly righted it. He wondered whether she was sleepy or whether the teetering was part of her shaking disease. He wondered what she could tell him about his father that he didn't know. He wondered what it would have been like to have a mother who had loved him, or even a mother who had talked.

After the movie ended Asim stood at the lobby door and nodded good-bye to the moviegoers. One of the last, the redhead, he hadn't noticed come in. Asim knew he had not sold him a ticket.

"I hope it's okay. I slipped in to see the last thirty minutes. Too early to go home alone, too late to stay at the Pig Iron and go home happy," the guy said.

"Thirty minutes. I guess you saw enough to whet your appetite."

"Yeah, but now I know the end. Besides I don't like 007 much, even though this one's got a pretty face."

"Right."

Asim fidgeted with the theater keys, but was enjoying the attention. Now just a foot away, the redhead said, "I see you in the park sometimes. You're always in a hurry."

Asim thought, *maybe he'll touch me.*

The guy handed him a page from the *Buffalo Options* personals. One of the ads was circled: *Only The Lonely. GWM, 30, Irish, pretty handsome, but no Adonis, looking for love. You: Egyptian, younger, nuts for the movies.*

The guy whispered, "Want to go to the park now?"

Sonia appeared just then and Asim turned to her; more nervous, he folded the newspaper page and put it in his pocket. He said, pointing at Sonia, "Sorry. I've got a date."

"Who's he?" she asked.

Asim was surprised she sounded angry.

"Someone testing out the movie," he said.

The guy gave Sonia a look, patted Asim on the shoulder, and

said, "Another time." He left, singing "Dum-dum-dum-dumdy-doo-wah."

Sonia said, loud enough for him to hear, "That's right, mumble like an idiot."

"It's part of a song," Asim said.

She gave him a look.

Billy Maguire, he remembered, that was his name. A few weeks earlier in the park, Asim had seen someone going down on him and watched from behind a tree until an old guy came up beside Asim and touched his ass, and said, "Yeah, Billy Maguire's cute. Too bad he's an Irish drunk." Asim ran away and didn't think Billy had noticed. But he had, and had tracked Asim to the theater.

Tony, the projectionist, came down from upstairs. "A wrap. Hey, Sonia, you look nasty, like the kids today say, nasty-fine."

"You think I don't know you're full of it," she said.

He gave her a hug.

"How's Masika?" he asked Asim. "Haven't seen much of her."

"She's doing doubles at Deaconess," Asim said.

"Need some help closing?"

"I can handle it."

Sonia said, "We'll miss Joseph."

"The usher?" Tony asked. "He's been dead for years, Sonia."

She ignored him.

"You want a ride?" Tony asked her.

She turned to Asim, who'd glanced over to the Pig Iron but then noticed her lost look. "I'll take her," he said.

He locked the last lobby door after the projectionist, and went back to Sonia.

"You liked the show?"

"That man's dangerous," she said.

"Tony?"

"No, the stupid scarlethead. Don't let him in the Bethlehem any-more."

Asim didn't know why she sounded so agitated, and said, "Fine. It's red."

"What?"

"His hair is red."

"*Goldfinger*'s my favorite. I saw it with Badru. He laughed so hard he dropped his Coca-Cola in his lap. He bought a bowler like Oddjob's, not as heavy."

He remembered seeing it in the closet, though he never saw his old man wear it.

"When did you meet my father?"

She took out a cigarette and tried to light it, but she was shaking too much. "That's a story for another night."

"What did you say when you left the car last week? Something like *razrishiti*. I tried to find out what it means and couldn't. Maybe I didn't spell it right, r-a-z-r-i-s-h-i-t-i."

"I say things I don't remember."

"But the word, what does it mean?"

"*Razrishiti?* It means *let me*," she said. "Maybe I was thinking of Gypsy Rose Lee, you know, *Everybody's got to have a gimmick, let me entertain you.*"

Her voice was creaky.

He didn't know Gypsy Rose Lee but he laughed when she tried to sing the song, which he'd recognized.

"I'm tired," she said. "I can't even sing a little song."

"You didn't come to his funeral."

"It was hard enough getting back here."

He could tell he was worrying her, and said, "Just a second."

He ushered her to a bench under a poster of King Kong perched atop the Empire State Building.

"I have to make the last check down the aisles and lock the emergency doors before we go."

"Take your time and do it right." She glanced back at the movie poster. "I saw this, too. Isn't he a beautiful monkey?"

"A gorilla."

"You think you know so much." Calmer, she managed to light the cigarette.

"I'll be right back."

Asim checked every row to make sure no one had fallen asleep and yelled, "lights out," in case he'd missed some drunk hunkering inside a seat. He locked the exits and checked the bathrooms. He grabbed his coat from the office. He pictured Billy Maguire in the woods with a guy on his knees and thought about how much he liked the reddish hair around the cocks of Irish kids in the gym showers. *Tarik would kill me if he knew,* he thought. An ad. Only The lonely. Maybe that was a little weird. Still he was surprised by how much he wanted the attention, and he thought Billy was pretty good-looking. He didn't believe Billy was a drunk. He heard Sonia coughing and returned to the lobby.

"You okay?" he asked.

"Too much smoke," she said, bending down to put out her cigarette on the marble floor.

"I'll toss that." He took the butt from between her fingers. She was trembling less than when she'd arrived. He walked over to the ash can and stuffed the butt into the sand.

"A cigarette makes my hand shake less," she said.

"I could tell."

He remembered the night's receipts in the safe—seven hundred dollars, pretty good for a midweek opener, and decided he'd return for the money in the morning.

"What do you say about a ride in my Aston-Martin?" he asked, taking her hand. He felt it tremor and grow calm inside his palm.

She surprised him by starting to hum Shirley Bassey's *Goldfinger*.

"You're a *knockout* tonight," he said, proud he'd found a word she'd appreciate.

"You're like all the rest." She winked.

When they got to the car, he looked to see if Billy Maguire had returned to the Pig Iron, but if he had, he wasn't watching from the window. The only sound was the music of the jukebox, a country-western song Asim had heard blaring out often before: "I was a good love/a good love gone bad/a good love gone bad/a good love gone bad." All night he'd hear the lyrics in his head.

On the way to Sonia's, he asked her again about his father.

She ignored him.

He wondered whether her head was filled with *good love gone bad*.

"We're here," he said, deciding to lay off the talk about his old man.

"I can see."

"So what did you think about the movie?"

"I don't like deserts."

"That makes two of us."

She said she loved that phrase, *two of us,* and leaned over and kissed his cheek.

He didn't know what to say, and thought, *Wait a minute. This is the woman my father loved.* He looked at her and thought, *Harold and Maude.* He smiled.

"I'm glad you're happy," she said.

He thought, *I guess I am. That's something.*

She opened the door before Asim could help her out. She tapped the passenger window, her fingers quivering. He leaned across the seat and opened it and felt her hand twitching on his arm.

"Be good, Asim, the protector."

"How do you know that's what my name means?"

"Your father told me."

She turned and climbed the stairs to the house and disappeared inside.

KALASHNIKOVS

TARIK STOOD OUTSIDE the glass doors of the mosque. Built of white cinderblocks, it was more a high school gymnasium than a place of worship, a white cupola rising incongruously from the flat roof. He was waiting with the others—Kamal Ferran and six Yemeni neighbors. A bus pulled up, and the imam, carrying a suitcase, stepped off. Everyone else stayed back while Ferran greeted the man, known only as Shamal, who had traveled from the Islamic Learning Center in Terre Haute. Tarik wished he had spent more time studying Arabic; he had heard the imam could recite the entire Koran from memory. A genuine Hafiz.

They stopped in the entrance and removed their shoes, which

they placed on an arched rack. Tarik paused when they passed the clocks showing the five times of daily prayer, and he saw that the imam had turned and noticed him. No one said a word. They entered the washroom to perform Wudu. Tarik sat before a sink beside Shamal but was careful not to look at the holy man while they cleansed themselves to prepare for prayers: First Tarik washed his right hand to the wrist and then his left; he gargled his mouth and throat with water and cupped his palms and filled them and let the water fall down his nose and face. He cleaned his arms up to the elbow, his right one first. He passed his wet hands over his head from his forehead to his neck, washed his ears, and finally bent down to spread water on his feet up to his ankles. Inside the heart of the mosque, the prayer hall was empty of decoration or furniture except for the floor carpet divided into individual prayer mats for worshipers. Shoeless, they sat cross-legged in a square. The others seemed restless, still undecided about whether it was worth giving up a night when the Sabres were playing at the hockey arena in Buffalo. *Idiots*, Tarik thought. *They don't want to learn about Mecca.* Before the imam said a word, he had passed out photographs of Ka'ba, which reminded Tarik of the monolith the ape-men watched rising out of the ground in *2001: A Space Odyssey*. He knew a good Muslim shouldn't enjoy the movies, and he bit down on his tongue, ashamed he couldn't stop remembering being inside the darkened Bethlehem Theater.

As he pictured Ka'ba in the heart of Mecca, he was embarrassed because a former Ukrainian church, no matter what you did to it, was no place to host Shamal. He hated the Ukes. They called his people *Arabians* and he knew they were thinking *towelheads* or *desert shits.* He didn't understand why Ferran invited this holy man here, to their house. There should be a proper mosque.

Tarik knew he was more admired than any of the other young Muslim men in Lackawanna. He had been told none of the elders would be at the evening prayer, only the seven young men, Ferran and the imam. Shamal, with a mystical voice, they were told, would be unfettered. Afterward they would go to Ferran's apartment and Tarik would learn what Allah expects. He was promised a meeting alone with the imam. Ferran had spoken to Shamal. Tarik thought, *I am one of the chosen.*

"Ever since the Ka'ba was built, good Muslims have battled in the name of Allah," Shamal said, fixing his eyes on each young man, one by one. "You've heard of Chechnya?"

They nodded, though Tarik knew they were clueless.

"I walked from the Dagestan border into Chechnya just a year ago. I killed four Russian pigs with one of their own Kalashnikovs."

No one stirred.

"Do you remember Khobar Tower?" he asked.

Again, they nodded and Tarik thought, *They know nothing.*

"It was our Pearl Harbor."

He asked, "Do you know any queers in town?"

Everyone looked surprised. Everyone except Tarik shook his head.

"In Egypt, there is a ship of debauchery called the *Queen Boat,* where men strip naked and commit *haran.* The faithful urge the police to arrest the deviants, some are punished with electric shock, others executed. They are almost as shameful as Jews. You have everything to learn."

Tarik fell unexpectedly sad and wished there was a way to save his brother. He looked back and saw Ferran was smiling. Tarik wondered if he knew about Asim, and thought how fat and self-satisfied the idiot looked. How could this holy man respect Ferran, someone who lived on Burger King? Tarik worried Ferran would use his brother against him.

Then the imam began the Salah, and after they were finished praying, everyone asked, one by one, for God's forgiveness and blessing.

Before leaving the mosque, Shamal said in English as riveting as *adhan:* "Pilgrimage to Mecca won't save you, only *jihad,* only sacrifice."

Tarik looked back and saw Ferran bowing east toward Mecca, and he thought, *I want to shoot Kalashnikovs.*

The six others walked the short distance to Ferran's apartment while Tarik lingered behind. Shamal pulled the sleeve of his coat and said, "Come with us."

The imam and Ferran spoke Arabic, and Tarik could only understand a single word, *haran,* which meant *forbidden.* He heard his name but didn't know what the imam was saying. The visitor put an arm through his, which was the Muslim tradition, and as they walked, clutched together, he worried the Ukes, if they noticed, would think: *faggots.* Ferran carried the suitcase, and about halfway there he tripped on a swell in the sidewalk. When the case struck the ground it opened, and though nothing spilled out, the imam cursed, or at least Tarik believed it was an Arabic curse, something he had heard his mother whisper about his father that he thought meant *idiot, numbskull, asshole.* In the light he saw bills, ten-dollar, maybe hundred-dollar ones. Shamal knelt and felt for something inside the case, and when he found it, the imam said something in

Arabic that relieved Ferran, who shut the case and then made sure the latch was fastened. For the last few blocks, nobody talked.

Ferran's third-floor apartment was near the Yemen Soccer Field, where the young men, except for Tarik, played in the all-season evening league. Ferran led them up the dim stairway, only a single light at the top of the stairs illuminating it. Shamal climbed ahead of Tarik, who noticed, for the first time, the imam was wearing boots like a mountain climber's. The three had arrived before the Yemenis, and Tarik wondered whether they'd been scared off; or maybe just got bored. They were worthless; he tried to remember in his head the Arabic curse he'd just heard, but couldn't. Instead he thought, *They're scum.* They reminded him of what Travis Bickle said about New York: "All the animals come out at night."

The Yemeni "boys"—that's what Ferran had stupidly taken to calling them—had stopped at the variety store and brought back beer, Cheetos, bags of vinegar potato chips. A week before, Ferran had told everyone to study the Israel massacre after the second Palestine Intifada. Tarik was ready: He had learned that Ariel Sharon, guarded by armed soldiers, had walked into the Al-Aqsa mosque in Jerusalem. Unarmed Palestinians protested, throwing rocks at the intruders. Seven martyrs were gunned down on the holy land. Call for *jihad* was obvious. If these Yemeni jerks knew anything, he'd be stunned. *Scum.*

On the wall above a worn leather couch where Shamal sat was a framed photograph of Manchester United left behind by a Pakistani from England who had rented the apartment before Ferran moved in. Sitting before the British soccer team, Shamal seemed out of place. His eyes were volcanic black, illuminated by a bare bulb on a nearby wall sconce. He was tall and lean and wore a square burgundy cotton cap. Tarik looked carefully at Shamal's cap. He knew where they were sold. He would get one tomorrow. The hair on the imam's chin was scraggly like a terrier's. Tarik thought, *I want to be like him.*

The youngest Yemeni, Mukhtar Al-Bakri, unpacked a carton of Genesee and Tarik cringed when the boy tore open the potato chip bags. He had noticed the imam's mouth twitch before Shamal shouted an invective in Arabic. Ferran rushed to the boy and gathered the beer and food in his arms and whisked them off to the kitchen. Shamal settled himself and reached into the suitcase at his feet for a loaf of thick-crusted round bread and a jar of honey.

"This is what the teachings of the *Tablighi Jamaat* say should nourish us: simple food, bread and lentils, tea and almonds."

Taqua, Tarik thought.

The imam broke off pieces of the bread with an intensity that impressed Tarik and passed them out.

"In a city with so many Arabs, no flatbread for sale." Shamal shrugged.

All the while the young men smoked—Winstons, Newports, Marlboros were scattered everywhere. The smoke made Tarik dizzy. The imam lit up Egyptian tobacco mixed with molasses and cherry. He chastised Ferran for not providing the communal pipe. The rebuke pleased Tarik. The sweet smell of Shamal's tobacco tamed the acrid, nervous odor of the American cigarettes. Surprising Tarik, the imam handed him a wood pipe the color of Jerusalem olive and, with a nod that made him feel more important than he had ever felt before, Shamal said, nearly whispering, *Allahu akbar.*

The others watched Tarik. Unaccustomed to smoking, he nonetheless inhaled deeply, feeling the smoke swarm into his lungs, and without a single tremor, he let the smoke drift from his mouth so slowly it seemed spectral in the air. It felt sexy. He worried his pleasure would offend Allah.

Shamal rose and clapped his hands once, startling everyone.

"Bring in the beer. A Muslim in America, even ones born here like all of you, is a traveler far from home and can indulge," the imam said.

Tarik breathed in another hit of Egyptian tobacco and pictured himself wearing military fatigues; Travis Bickle in a black-and-white checkered head scarf. A Kalashnikov close to his side in the Bethlehem Theater. The last showing of the night playing, some stupid Danny DeVito movie, something like *What's the Worst That Can Happen.* Ten, twenty people inside. Before he wasted them, he would shout, "I'll show you a *towelhead,*" and then the short bursts, until everyone was dead. He would look for the Russian bitch his father had fucked and stand over her and wait long enough before firing so that she would see him when he pressed the trigger. Maybe by then Asim would realize the gunfire wasn't coming from the movie and run to the top of the carpet. Tarik would walk up to his brother and say, "Don't follow father to the grave." He would show mercy in the name of Allah, and for the last time walk calmly out of the movie house. He imagined Asim giving up a taste for men and rushing to join him.

Ferran returned, tapped Tarik on the shoulder, and handed him the first long-necked bottle of Genesee. Tarik wasn't sure what was happening. He didn't want to take the beer but believed Shamal must have known what he was doing. The others remained cross-legged on the floor as if still at evening prayers and looked stupid, one in a Buffalo Bills jersey, another in a T-shirt emblazoned with a loud-mouthed Homer Simpson, and someone in a red jacket with a huge 8-ball painted across the back. Tarik wore a black turtleneck.

"Tea is weak on a night like this for a message that will bring you to Mecca," the imam said.

He reached into the suitcase and removed a skull, and after cradling it he placed it on the ratty trunk Ferran used for a coffee table. Balak, the meekest, gasped. Shamal emptied ash into the bony cavity, and fattened his pipe bowl with more sweet tobacco.

He spoke in Arabic, which sentence by sentence, Ferran translated:

"Here is the skull of a Jew. Don't be afraid to kill a non-Muslim; be glad especially to kill a Zion son. This Jew was exploded by a martyr much younger than any of you. In Israel, Zion boys are told to rip out the fetus from the womb of a Palestinian and carve out the skull for an ashtray. So, you see, we are not the monsters. Do not be afraid to kill a Jew. It is what can save you. It is *jihad*."

THREE'S COMPANY

THE SCARLETHEAD who had spoiled their time in the lobby—Sonia had his number. She knew what Asim was thinking when that bum patted the boy on the shoulder and said, "Another time." *He's too young to have a boyfriend*, she thought. *Besides, he could do a lot better than this guy.* She hoped that he loved girls too. He was so much like his father she could cry. She had to admit to herself that the guy was handsome, and except for the red hair he looked a little like Gary Cooper. She used to love the actor, even though he wasn't anything like her Nicholas. He wasn't dark and brooding. She liked to imagine Cooper walking into a saloon in a place with a name like Tombstone. In a corner, he spotted a bar girl sitting with a gold miner, and of course she smiled when she saw him push through the swinging doors. Anyone could tell he was thinking: *She's mine. The only woman for a hundred men and she's mine.* Sonia shook her head and thought, *The boy's mine.* After she saw Gary Cooper walk into the saloon, Sonia sometimes pretended she was the bar girl in Tombstone. She sailed up the stairs into a lacy bedroom, undressed carefully, and dabbed perfume on her arms and neck. She lay on the bed against a pile of pillows while Gary Cooper, his eyes shimmering in the lamplight, stood before her. He would have been gentle, even though he could have easily killed a man and like other desperadoes, be killed, too. Nicky could probably kill someone. But Badru wouldn't hurt anybody. The boy, he's gentler than them all. She saw the scarlethead look at Asim the way Gary Cooper looked at the woman and she knew she had to warn the kid that the man is just a Lackawanna deadbeat. He's nothing like Gary Cooper or Nicky or the boy's father. The Pig Iron bum will only hurt him. She remembered what Badru had told her, just weeks before he died: "I worry about Asim, my son, the protector."

She had to sit to take off her sweater. When it stuck under her chin, she yanked so hard her hands quaked and felt like they would snap off. She had nearly fallen back onto the bed before she pulled it over her head. She braced her fidgety hands on the mattress and with one foot kicked off a shoe, and bending over, removed the other. Undressing had become so arduous. Her toes were bunched into the tip of her nylons like small body parts packed into a bell jar at the freak show. She remembered her father had forced her into the tent when she was young. The jars—a little bigger than the Ma-

son ones her mother filled with pickled beets and pigs' feet—were
stacked on a table next to a dwarf woman with a dead grassy beard
falling from her chin and a smile so tight it looked sewn on. Even
then, she thought, *How can he take his daughter here?*

Now, she raised herself, reached inside her dress, slid her panty-
hose from her hips to her ankles and worked them off. She stared
at her veins. Her legs—a stringy mess. She slipped the top of her
dress down one shoulder at a time until she could pull each arm out.
She stood, and let the dress fall into a bundle on the floor. She didn't
remove her silk panties because the cloth felt sexy against her skin.
She was too tired to wash the makeup from her face. She walked to
the bureau and picked out a flannel nightdress and returned to the
bed. In her unsteady hands it rippled as she held it over herself. She
slipped it on as best she could. The night was colder than it should
have been, *"colder than a witch's tit,"* her father used to say. She
hated the phrase. *Wife beater,* she thought. She was determined not
to raise the thermostat. She used to like a cool room before she had
grown so old. *My blood,* she thought, *isn't warm like it used to be.
I'm getting more amphibious every day. Throw me in the sea.*

She got into bed. Lying on her side, she could see the red neon
from the DB Mart splash onto the floor. Her head started shaking.
She didn't want to be sixty-eight years old. Or maybe she meant
she didn't want to be sick and sixty-eight. She wasn't sure. She
didn't want to be this old alone. She had heard death rattling somewhere. She wondered why men were threatening. She wished more
could be like Asim. *The boy is the one who needs to be protected.
I don't trust the scarlethead,* she thought. She understood a man
could grow unsatisfied with a love. She could forgive her father for

his faithlessness, but she could never forgive his violence. She pictured the scarlethead stalking the boy with a gun as if she were watching it all in an old '40s movie. Every part of her, it seemed, trembled terribly.

Soon, it would be one in the morning, and she knew she wasn't going to sleep. She lay on her hands to try to quell the shaking, and after she had calmed enough to know that her body would not fail her, she got out of bed. At the closet near the front door she struggled into her wool coat. She thought, *Shoes, I need shoes.* She sat on a chair and bent over and shoved her feet into her white Keds. She thought about lacing them, but let the strings dangle. *Socks,* she thought, but she decided taking off the sneakers and putting everything back on was more than she could handle. She left her apartment and walked half a block on Wilkesbarre to the house on Holland where she was born. Her shaking was indistinguishable from shivering. She sat on a bench in the backyard. The stump her mother had rested on after a fight with her father was gone. She looked up to her parents' bedroom window and muttered that they knew nothing about love. She said—loud enough to scare away a prowling skunk—"you miserable whore master." She knew it was a terrible thing to say about a father, but she didn't care. *Why couldn't my mother have been more like Judy Holliday. Why couldn't she find a man who loved her? Why did she let herself be born yesterday?* she thought.

A light went on inside the house, and minutes later a police car arrived. Sgt. Peter Pelligrino—she'd known him for years—walked up and sat beside her.

"Mrs. Markovich, what are you doing here?"

"I couldn't sleep."

"It's cold. Are you okay?"

"I'm old."

Pelligrino smiled, and after a while, he said, "You don't live here anymore."

"I know. My name used to be Salvaggio."

"What?" the cop asked.

"I changed it back to Markovich when Nicky died." She thought, *I was so mad at him.*

"Come on, I'll take you home. You can't keep sitting in a stranger's backyard. Some night I'll have to write you up."

She wondered what in the world he had meant by that, *write you up,* but she wasn't in the mood to find out and didn't say anything more until the cruiser was stopped outside her house. She thought about the Bond movie.

"*The World Is Not Enough,*" she said.

"You're telling me."

She patted Pelligrino's shoulder the way a toddler does with someone she loves.

"Sweet boy," she said.

"Charming won't help you next time, Mrs. Markovich."

She could tell he was joking, and she raised her brow, closed an eye, and said, "Here's looking at you, kid."

But he was a disappointment because he never got the movie references, not even Bogart.

She saw him from the window, waiting outside until she switched on the light. She let her coat fall into the bundle with her dress and sweater. She kicked off her sneakers, glad she didn't have to bend to unlace them. She noticed the daguerreotype of her mother and grandfather on the mantel. (It was next to a Polaroid of Nicky and Badru.) The dusky photo was taken before Anna and Alexander boarded a ship in Riga, in 1915, to Canada. Her grandfather was a kind man like Badru and Asim. He wasn't tragic like Nicky.

"Don't worry, men can be kind, honey. All men aren't angry like your father," her mother once told her.

Sonia's mother was fourteen when she arrived in Canada; she wore a plain kerchief over her head. Her face was diamond-shaped, bright, with a shouting smile. She held her father's arm. His shoulders spread out like thick bends in a tree, while he leaned on a cane and the polished piece of birch that was his right leg shone. His eyes were pensive. When he laughed, her mother had told her, his great white beard shook. It was during the crossing on the ocean liner *Mongolia* that Anna had met Sergei Markovich, and they married months later.

Decades passed, her father was dead, and Sonia remembered sitting beside her mother, who had been stricken with the same shaking disease that now was claiming her. The old woman couldn't sleep, and feverish, she cursed the man who had become her husband, yelling out "*bastard*" and scratching at the air.

"I hated him, too," Sonia whispered.

The old woman gave her daughter a look and described how under a prickly blanket, swaying with the motion of the Atlantic under them, he had entered her for the first time.

"I was fourteen," she said, momentarily lucid in her delirium.

She said that she was frightened because it had hurt as he pushed himself into her. Nearby someone was moaning. "Was it the girl from Latvia?" She had raised her voice and grabbed her daughter's hand. "He was a filthy boy even then," she said, remembering that he pushed himself in harder and harder. "He was driving me into the sea. Your father was a pig."

Sonia was crying, but her mother was so lost in the past she hadn't noticed.

Overtaken by her dreaminess, the old woman described a bear crawling into her room sometimes and climbing into bed so that she could pet the length of its fur. She said she breathed harder as she felt the bear, hunkered beside her. She said the animal smelled like birch bark and earth. The bear wasn't anything like her husband, who slumped off after sex without a word of kindness and smelled like shit. She asked Sonia to lean in close and whispered, "Your father couldn't fuck a cow."

Sonia didn't know what to say.

That night, after her mother's delirium had calmed and the old woman slept, Sonia left the bedside and sat in the living room before an open window, the air pungent with the odor of burning iron ore. She imagined that she was with Badru and Nicky, naked, in bed. She held her lips against her husband's neck and swirled her tongue against the knotty bone where his chest began. She told him to turn because she loved pressing her sex against his ass. She kissed his ear and whispered, "Down there," touching her sex, but she could tell he didn't have his heart in it. She hoisted herself over him, and slid far enough away so that she could cup her chin in her palm. She watched the two men kiss and tumble. *Three's company*, she thought. *Sabrina and her lovers.*

The television brought her back from her reverie. She hadn't even realized that she'd left it on. Ralph Kramden made a fist and told Alice he was going to send her to the moon. Outside the window, the moon hung like a white parenthesis in the sky. She remembered Neil Armstrong in a space suit and bubble helmet and an American flag in his hand, walking lugubriously on the moon. Atop the television was a photograph of Nicholas and Badru, a close-up, shoulder-to-shoulder, arm across arm. They were happy. They were always happier together. She remembered when she took the Polaroid that they smiled sweetly, just after she had made them say, "*Love me.*"

Sonia looked out to the DB Mart neon and thought, *If only time hadn't stolen everything.*

She remembered the redhead. She could tell he was shit. She thought, *I'll tell Asim the redhead is trouble. I'll tell him the redhead is shit like my father. I'll make sure he understands about bad love. It's like that song, a good love gone bad. A good love always goes bad.* She surprised herself by what she thought next: *I wish I could see the boy naked.* And then she thought of how angry Badru would be.

LIGHTS OUT

WHEN ASIM GOT HOME, all the lights were out. He remembered that his sister was working the nightshift.
He walked upstairs and noticed Tarik's door ajar. There was enough
light from the street so that he could tell no one was in-side. One of
the few times he had ever been alone in the room, he turned on a
lamp clamped to the headboard and saw, on the desk, the note someone had taped to the Bethlehem door: "Okay, towelheads, open up
the show." Asim was surprised that his brother had kept it. There
was a drawing of hooded stick figures hanging, execution-style,
from trees and a bowling-ball bomb with a fuse dangling from its
top. There was a postcard-size note with the heading: "DON'T BE

FOOLED BY THESE ARABS: Christa McAuliffe, astronaut; Doug Flutie, NFL quarterback; Cindy Lightner, MADD founder; Jacques Nasser, Ford Motor CEO; Helen Thomas, White House correspondent." Tarik had written in: "Badru Zahid, movie house fool." Below the names in bold letters: "WE DO NOT ASSIMILATE." He sat on the bed and noticed a pamphlet on the edge near a pillow, with three Arab children, two boys and a girl, on the cover. He opened it, and at the top was this invitation: "*ADOPT A MARTYR'S CHILD*: *For $50 a month a child of Shuhada could be given a life fitting for the sacrifice of a martyred parent. Imagine the clothes and sweets, the smiles a donation could bring such a parentless child.*" He heard a car pull in, and when he reached to shut off the light, the note and everything else fell to the floor. He groped for them in the dark and hurriedly put everything back. At the window he watched his brother get out of the back seat. He had seen the car before outside the mosque, a rusted Volvo that Tarik had borrowed. It belonged to Kamal Ferran, the "fat shit Yemeni," his father used to say. "What does your brother see in the bastard? What does he see in Islam?"

When Tarik leaned into the window of the car to talk to someone, Asim bolted and reached his room before he heard the front door open. He sat on his bed, breathless, hoping Tarik had not noticed the light go out. He heard footsteps on the stairs and tried to think what he would say if Tarik stormed into his room.

Why do you call the old man a movie house fool? he would shout back.

He heard his brother's door creak and shut. He heard a bureau drawer sliding. It was that quiet.

Pajamas, he thought. Tarik never slept naked.

Even years ago, before his brother knew he was gay, Tarik told him: "When you shower with other boys at school, you shame your family."

Tarik walked back down the hallway to the bathroom. Asim heard water running in the sink. The toilet flushed. He imagined his brother bare-chested like Renard in the 007 movie, but even more handsome. He listened for the bed springs. He heard chanting in Arabic. And after a few minutes, there was silence, and he knew Tarik had fallen asleep.

He decided he would convince Masika that they had to do something. She was wrong. They couldn't just let their brother go.

Asim stood and unbuckled his pants and let them fall to his ankles. He slid his briefs down and stepped out of them. He unbuttoned his shirt and threw it onto the chair. He sat and removed his socks. He admired his nakedness and knew he had grown into a body that a man—his new older guy with red hair—would love to touch. He felt the shock of the cold sheet when he slipped his legs under the covers. He shivered and thought of Sonia shaking. He pictured Billy Maguire, naked and muscular, the smell of beer and tobacco. He touched himself and whispered, "Dumdy-doo-wah." He thought, *What does Sonia know about this redhead? Who does she think she is, telling me what to do?* He pictured Tarik, strong and handsome. He wished he were that rugged. He remembered the airline ticket. He remembered Sonia saying, "Asim, the protector." He didn't believe it. He was just lonely in Lackawanna.

THE TEA KETTLE HISSING

WHEN SONIA AWOKE, it was so cold she could stay out of bed just long enough to ignite the gas burner under the tea kettle. She climbed back under the covers and turned to the window to see what the day looked like: Frozen, the fifth straight day without sun and still no snow. She thought she might have to break down and raise the thermostat. Her back ached and the bottom of her feet burned and tingled. Sometimes when she flexed the right foot, it felt as if a knife were slicing the sole. She raised her arm and watched it tremble like a part of a body before death snatches it. She wondered how so much could have been lost and wanted something, *anything*, back. She looked at the digital alarm that Badru had given her years ago and was surprised it was so late: nine o'clock already. The clock was shaped like the shoe in *The Gold Rush*. She didn't remember what time she'd fallen asleep. She didn't remember going to her old house down the street or the cop who had taken her home. She barely remembered Asim. She was still half asleep, dreaming of the little tramp lost in Alaskan tundra where bears froze and cracked apart. She remembered him running from a devouring giant, every gesture an escape and laughter. She had seen all of his films. The tramp dressed in the same black dusty suit, lonesomeness faded into it, and still he bobbled back and forth beyond misery. She wondered if the little tramp imagined marrying a beautiful Italian actress, someone like Maria Bertini, her hair dark and curly, surrounded by a fluffy boa red as poppies. He would understand the twitching of an old woman sick with the shaking disease. Sometimes when she caught a glimpse of herself trembling in the mirror, she would see the sad-faced actor shuffling back and forth on the sides of his shoes as if a flickering motion were the way a body rouses right out of itself. He would teach her to dance so that every part of her shook with the rhythm that people wouldn't say was sick and crazy. They would dance outside the Bethlehem until a crowd gathered. The little tramp would disappear, and in his place would be Nicky and Badru. Asim would be watching. Nothing bad would matter because they would dance right out of their bodies.

She nearly fell asleep, but the sound of the tea kettle heating to a boil roused her. She remembered that the only movie she had seen with her mother and father was the matinee *You Can't Take It with You*, when she was six. She didn't know it then, but her mother had hoped the romance and humor would soften her father. *She* hoped her father later that night wouldn't hit her mother, but she was wrong. She was wrong about this most of the time. She heard the tea kettle whistling, but she couldn't stop remembering Jimmy Stewart and Jean Arthur and how she wished they could have been her parents because Stewart, who wouldn't hurt anyone in a million years, made her laugh. Her father seldom made her even smile. When the movie was over, her father didn't say a word. He went to the Pig Iron, while she and her mother walked home. They stopped and lit a candle at Our Lady of Victory. She remembered thinking her mother was as beautiful as the Madonna in the painting above the votive table, and all the while watching a flickering candle, she prayed that her father would never come home again. Later that night, alone in bed, she listened for him. He screamed something about the fuckin' Irish in the town, and then she heard it: the slap across her mother's face. Just one, no more. Most nights there was only one. And then she thought she heard something different. It sounded like her father sobbing. The next morning he had already left for the mill by the time she came downstairs, and her mother tried to smile when she appeared in the kitchen. In the morning, her mother always tried to smile, but Sonia, even then, when she was ten, knew there wasn't much to be happy about.

Now, she lifted her head and listened. The tea kettle was hissing on the stove, but she was too tired to get up and closed her eyes for a few minutes, no more, she promised herself. She wished her mother could have been happy, and thought, *Why couldn't the Little Tramp have been in love with her? Why couldn't Jimmy Stewart have whisked her away? Why couldn't she have been saved like a girl in the movies?*

ARABIC GIBBERISH

ASIM WOKE ABOUT EIGHT. His neck ached. He pulled off the blanket and sheet, sat on the edge of the bed, and looked at his hard-on. He closed his eyes and saw Billy Maguire; his brother in the driveway, waving good-bye to bearded men in dark robes; Sonia shaking. Everything looked as if he were watching from inside a silent avalanche.

On the way to the shower, with only a towel in his hand, his brother stopped him.

"You insist on shaming yourself and your family," Tarik said. "Allah orders that no one, not even a brother, should see another's nakedness. A man should always be covered from his navel to his knees."

Asim wanted to say something like *fuck you and the Allah you woke up with*. Instead he put the towel around his waist, but his brother wasn't finished.

"A *sura* says *do not take your fathers and your brothers for guardians if they love unbelief more than belief.* "

"Don't you get it? I don't care," Asim said. "Listen, I know there's something wrong."

Tarik wasn't listening. Asim wondered whether he was high.

"You ever hear of a nightclub in Cairo called Queen Boat?"

"No."

"Faggots go there."

Asim tried hard not to look nervous. He almost said he knew about the ticket to Islamabad, but his brother held his arm so tight it hurt.

"In Egypt, the police can castrate a fag." Tarik let go, lifted his hand, and sliced the air between them. "Swish," he said.

"Masika's right. Maybe we should forget about you." Asim was trying hard to control himself.

"Father was a fag too."

"Fuck you."

Asim didn't know what to expect. A punch in the stomach. A kick in the groin.

His brother smiled and said, "We'll see."

He started to walk away, and Tarik held him back. "Wait . . . *Al-laumma in-nee a'oothu bika minal khubu-thee wal khabaa ith.*"

"What's that? Some desert curse?"

"It's what a good Muslim says when entering the toilet."

Asim shook his head, stepped past Tarik into the bathroom, and locked the door. He let the towel fall to the floor. He thought: *Masika's right. He's crazy. If I don't do something, he's going to cut off my balls.*

While he showered he pictured Egyptian men on the Queen Boat sailing the Nile under an endless, starry sky. *Corona Borealis, Orion, Hercules, Lupus.* Men danced, held hands, kissed. They were young and old, beautiful and dark. On the docks waiting for the boat were cops, dressed in khaki, clubs and guns at their sides, while in a barren prison station room doctors in white robes, holding scalpels, waited for the wagon from the dock to roll in. *Fuck Tarik,* he thought. This was his mother's Egypt. She could have it.

He lowered the showerhead so that the spray might loosen a knot in his neck that felt like a gear grinding into him. He didn't want to hate Tarik. He remembered the time his brother pretended to be Jackie Gleason's chef of the future. Tarik, dressed in their father's barbecue apron and feigning stage fright, said, *yiminie, yiminie, yiminie, oh, can you core an apple.* Asim was five and he laughed until his stomach hurt. His brother lifted him from the sofa and propelled him back onto the cushion and fell on top of him, tickling him furiously until he had to say, "man from uncle." His brother repeated, "say 'man from uncle' or you die."

Asim turned off the shower and dried himself, wrapped the towel around his waist, and tried to remember when his brother had become crazy. In high school, Tarik didn't have friends. Instead of going to college he read all day and rented movies at night. He used

to say, "I don't like the crowds at the Bethlehem." He loved reading history—Ancient Greece and Rome, Genghis Khan, Adolf
Hitler. Reigns of terror fascinated him. Asim thought, *I should have
known something was wrong.* On his way back to the bedroom he
paused outside his brother's door and listened. He heard chanting.
More Arabic gibberish, he thought.

OUT OF THE PAST

*S*ONIA AWOKE TO the dog's relentless barking crowding out her sleep, and then came the pounding on the front door, a wail of sirens, a metallic smell in the air. She sat up and could see smoke billowing from the stove, and for the first time that morning, she understood she wasn't dreaming. The smoke blackened. Her apartment was going to burn down.

She screamed, "Help." *That's what you do,* she thought, *you scream help.*

She covered her mouth with the end-table doily, not noticing the lacy pattern's holes that made it useless for a filter. She put her feet to the floor, knelt on all fours, and crawled—deliberately, low to the ground, beneath the thickest smoke. She coughed but just faintly. Smoke curled inside her chest. She reached up, undid the lock, and when the door opened, she was face to face with Gabriel, panting.

A firefighter ran past and yelled for everybody to get out.

Her neighbor Gordon lifted her to her feet and took her arm.

Inside the apartment, there was a small explosion, a pop really, and then a larger one. More firefighters rushed past. She stopped in the chaos: A stream of men in leather boots, hoods, helmets with air tanks on their backs, carrying axes, iron tools she didn't recognize and extinguishers. For a moment she thought she was dreaming again. Then she remembered, and said, "The tea kettle, it was the tea kettle, hissing."

"Let's go, Sonia," said Gordon, uncharacteristically insistent.

A firefighter stopped them on the stairway and led them out to the street. Already, neighbors swarmed.

She coughed vigorously and the cold gave her shivers that made her shaking look like she was on the way to some epileptic seizure. A stranger tried to put his coat around her shoulders, but a couple of men in uniforms whisked her off to a stretcher, while Gordon was pleading, "She's okay, she shakes all the time."

They weren't listening and told her to lie down and carted her into an ambulance.

"Where are you taking me?" she asked. "Call Asim."

She could see out a small window like a cruise ship porthole and thought that in the crowd she recognized the Arab who had glared at her on the bus. She thought she had seen Tarik.

"To Deaconess. You're going to be all right. What's your name, honey?" asked a woman who was hooking her up to a monitor.

"Don't call me '*honey*,'" she said. And then, "Who's that?"

"Who?"

"That miserable Arab."

"Now, honey, you live in *Arabian* town, you should know."

"Was there anyone next to him? Call Asim," she repeated just before the woman fitted an oxygen mask over her mouth and nose.

"No resuscitator?" asked someone else she hadn't noticed at first.

"The mask's enough," the woman said.

The pure oxygen felt cold and clean. It tickled at first, then made her throat dry, filled her lungs so that she didn't have to struggle for breaths. Her coughing ceased. She wished she knew someone in the ambulance and thought, *It's okay, I told them to call Asim.* She smiled.

"Happy, honey?" the woman asked.

Sonia thought '*honey*' isn't so bad after all. She nodded.

"You were really lucky."

She didn't feel lucky. She wondered whether everything she owned would be charred and was surprised that she didn't care about losing much, except for the photos in a box under her bed, a metal butter-cookie box, and she hoped the pictures would survive: her mother and grandfather crossing on the *Mongolia*. Her father cut out of every family photograph so that all that was left of him was a silhouette hole. Nicky and Badru, shoulder to shoulder, with the Niagara roaring behind them. She was glad she hadn't used a dress box like she had for her movie stubs. The tickets would be burnt for sure.

"You want to say anything, honey? I can lift the mask so you can talk."

"No," she said, in a voice like static through tiny punctures in the plastic.

"I understand. Just breathe in deeply and count in your head seven, six, five, four, three, two, one, when you let it out. It's soothing, isn't it?"

She did what the woman said and started drifting. Through the little window, she saw it had begun to snow. She remembered a story her mother had told her about old Russia. It was a peasant tale, her mother said: Once upon a time an ancient husband and wife lived in a snowbound cabin and sat before frosted windows. They scratched the glass clean to see snow spirits swirling outside among the birches. They were caretakers of the forest. In winter they worshiped fire and harsh wind. They said Our Lady of Tenderness hid out underneath the roots of a birch tree. Sometimes during a storm a witch would enter their house for a glass of tea. Restored by the kindness of the old couple, she returned to the forest and all night howled a witch's blessing. Our Lady of Tenderness never emerged.

"You should try to stay awake, honey," the woman said.

"I don't sleep much."

"You can rest at the hospital."

She didn't want to disappoint the woman who had called her honey. She kept her eyes open and smiled. In her mind she was mixing up all of her mother's stories: Outside a white-tailed deer foraged for pigwart and wild bloodroot. All night the sounds of coyotes barking, as if in a language of accusation, scouring the forest. Some voices in the forest cursed Our Lady. No use running for buckets, the forest was ablaze. The tea kettle hissed. She saw her grandfather's peg leg ignite. She saw the flames shooting from the stacks of Bethlehem Steel.

"Honey," the woman said.

Sonia was crying. She nodded, and as the ambulance pulled up to the hospital bay, her voice creaked through the mask: "It was hissing."

The woman stayed inside the ambulance while two orderlies, *fat and sloppy*, Sonia thought, wheeled her inside the building on a gurney. She had been to Deaconess a hundred times before, but never like this, by rescue on a bed with wheels. She had been there to see one neurologist after another, who would say there wasn't anything except drugs that could help her cope with shaking. She had liked the men. *They were handsome*, she thought, *not fat and sloppy*. She had forgotten their names, even the one she had been seeing for the past year. She would need to take her pills soon. She would need to eat toast with them or else she'd feel sick. What were the doctors' names?

Masika was the first nurse to meet the gurney.

"My god, Sonia," she said.

"Who are you?"

"Masika."

"I'm so sorry."

"Sorry?"

"I should have been there," she said, thinking about Badru's funeral.

"Where?"

"They say the day you die your name is written on a cloud."

"What?"

"It's from a movie your father loved, about a good man that can't get out of everything bad."

"You're mixed up, Sonia."

"*Out of the Past*. Every year in February, after Nicky died, Badru would make it a bonus second feature."

Masika guided them into another room, where another nurse was waiting.

"Oxygen?" she asked.

"Let's check her vitals first," Masika said.

"I have vitals?" Sonia asked.

"Can you breathe okay?"

Sonia nodded, while Masika took her arm and lifted it just enough so she could wrap a blood pressure cuff around it.

"I love your brother," Sonia said.

Masika looked surprised but didn't say anything.

The other nurse asked her name but she didn't answer.

"Sonia Markovich," Masika said. "We have to take good care of her."

Sonia smiled and said, "The tea kettle was hissing."

A doctor came in. Sonia thought he looked like the Arab on the bus. He wore thick Coke-bottle glasses.

"No," she screamed. "Get him away."

"Calm down, Sonia. He's a good doctor. He's going to help you," Masika said.

"Is Tarik with him?"

"Tarik? Why would he be here?"

She realized the doctor wasn't the Arab stranger and said, "I'm so stupid."

"Are you confused?" the doctor asked.

She didn't answer.

While he was checking her heart, Masika explained, "She has Parkinson's. The stress is making her condition worse."

"My pills," Sonia said.

"We'll take care of that," the doctor said.

She thought he had a sweet voice and felt even worse for her outburst.

"Blood pressure's normal," Masika said.

"No discernible lung problems, but we'll order an X-ray work-up just in case," the doctor said.

"X-ray. Like Superman," Sonia said. "Wasn't it awful how he fell off a horse?"

They laughed.

"It's not funny. He's a nice man."

"Christopher Reeves?" the doctor asked.

Surprised, she didn't know what to say. The doctor didn't look like a movie buff.

He took Masika aside and whispered something Sonia couldn't make out.

"She's a family friend," she heard Masika say.

The doctor came back, patted Sonia's leg, smiled, and left for another room.

"He winked at you," Sonia said.

"All eyes, aren't we? I can see you're going to be fine," Masika said.

Sonia reached out, her hand trembling in the space between them.

"I didn't want to miss your father's funeral. I didn't want to upset anybody."

"I knew that."

"I forgot to remember," Sonia said.

Masika looked bewildered.

"You're even prettier in white," Sonia said. "An angel."

"You're hallucinating."

"Your father used to say you looked like Judy Garland when she was young."

"Hm mmm."

"Did he tell you anything about me?" Sonia asked.

"Maybe we can talk about that another time." Masika ran her hand across Sonia's forehead.

Sonia decided she didn't care whether Badru ever talked about her. He had enough trouble with the Sinai crazy.

"You never knew my husband, Nicky."

"I think you should rest, Sonia."

Another patient was being wheeled in, and Sonia heard Masika's name being paged through pinholes in the ceiling.

"I think Asim has seen too much. We've got to make sure he doesn't get lost. Every boy needs a mother," Sonia said.

"Don't fret about him. He's pretty private, but stronger than you'd think. I've got to go, but I'll come back soon."

"I don't know how I live without them," she said, in a voice too low for anyone to hear.

The speaker pinholes sent out more static. She closed her eyes, shivered, and wished Masika had placed a blanket over her. The hospital sheet smelled of too much bleach. She heard something nearby crash and thought of *The Lady from Shanghai*. She remembered mirrors shattering into tiny pieces. She wondered whether Badru's wife believed she was conniving. She didn't care what that woman thought. She didn't give a shit about Tarik. The boy was enough to worry about. She missed Badru and Nicky. She wasn't conniving, ever, no *femme fatale*. She was in love. She remembered one of the first things she said to Badru; it was 1960 and he was watching Nicky in the concession line: "I know a lot of smart guys and a few honest ones. And you're both." He told her he knew where the line came from and she didn't make a very good Jane Greer, even though she was just as pretty. He was a good flirter too. She saw his look when Nicholas arrived and understood he didn't just care about a pretty woman flirting with him.

He said, "We're playing the movie game, remember *Out of the Past*, what Kirk Douglas's thug said about Greer: 'A dame with a rod is like a guy with a knitting needle.'"

Nicholas was confused but laughed anyway.

Badru said, "And what about Robert Mitchum: 'It was the bottom of the barrel and I scraped it. But I didn't care. I had them.'"

Sonia said, "I think you meant, her, had *her*, had Jane Greer."

Badru winked, and looking at them, said, *had you, both of you*."

Then he said: "Remember what Mitchum told her when he arrived in Mexico: 'I could go down to the cliff and look at the sea like a good tourist, but it's no good if there isn't somebody you can turn to and say, 'Nice view, huh. . . . Nothing in the world is any good unless you can share it.'"

He patted them both on the shoulders, and said, "Find a seat; you don't want to miss the opening."

She remembered how Nicky had turned around, and later whispered in her ear, "That guy, he winked at me."

She said, "I think he winked at *us*, baby."

That was the day everything started.

She opened her eyes and heard the blips and pings from her hospital room machinery. She palmed her cheek and realized her eyes had started to tear. The kettle, she remembered, the kettle was hissing.

GOD IS MISERY

ASIM DROVE TO THE theater to pick up the ticket sales he had left in the safe the night before. There was no sun, and clouds gathering over Lake Erie finally packed squalls. He loved the lake-driven snow, which his father said blew in like the storms in *Zhivago*. Every winter, the Bethlehem reprised the movie, drawing the city's Slavic immigrants. Asim liked to imagine himself growing into someone as beautiful as Omar Sharif. He used to think, *An Egyptian playing a Russian doctor and poet with a heart for endless love . . . maybe there's hope for a Muslim after all.* Now, he wondered about the first time Sonia would have seen *Zhivago*. Did his father walk her home in swirling snow, share a bottle of wine or jar of vodka, imagine Lackawanna as a Varykino ice palace? Was Nicholas there? He remembered the last time he watched the movie—the final showing of the weekend—only a handful of people in the house. Omar Sharif was talking to Rod Steiger about Julie Christie:

"What happens to a girl like that when a man like you is finished with her?" Sharif asked.

"You interested? I give her to you," Steiger said.

His father sighed, and muttered, "Bastard."

About a minute later the old man interrupted the movie—something he rarely did—and said, "You know, he isn't Muslim."

"Sharif?" Asim whispered.

"He's Coptic. He converted to marry. He was a fool. It didn't take long before he renounced Islam. He gave it all up."

Asim said, "So what."

The old man ignored him and said, "I was born a Muslim. But I don't care about that shit anymore. God is misery. I'd still be a prisoner to religion if I hadn't met them."

"Them?" Asim asked.

"Shhh," his father said, as if he had been the one who started talking. "Watch, this scene is beautiful."

On the screen in Technicolor's lush inlays of cyan, yellow, and magenta a snowbound train plowed endlessly through the Ural Mountains.

When he arrived at the movie house, Ferran's beat-up Volvo was parked in front. *Tarik,* he thought, *why would he be here?* Asim considered returning later because he didn't want a confrontation, especially with the zealot there. But his brother had noticed the Cadillac and ran out, waving for him to come inside.

Ferran was standing next to King Kong and, with his thickly-bearded chubby jowls, he looked ridiculous in a black jubbah. Another Muslim, a tall, lean man in a burgundy cap and white robe, was peering at the *Memento* coming-attractions poster. All that was visible was Guy Pearce's stare and the bridge of the actor's nose. The stranger was reading the tease: "The world doesn't just disappear when you close your eyes. Leonard Shelby is bent on revenge. He's searching for his wife's killer. What makes it hard: he can't make new memories."

The stranger turned and said, "*Memento mori*. It's one of the Latin phrases I've always respected."

"Tarik, what's going on?" Asim asked.

"That's no way to address your elder brother, when I bring guests," he said.

Ferran nodded, turned to the imam, and said, "American Muslim boys have a lot to learn."

"Asim, I want you to meet a holy man," his brother said, an apprehensive crick in his voice.

Asim extended his hand.

"No," his brother said. "You do not shake the hand of an imam. You bow."

"I don't bow, or curtsy—" Asim started to say, but he felt the sting of Tarik's palm on his face before he could finish.

"Fuck, Tarik. Who do you think you are?"

The stranger pulled Tarik aside and whispered something in his ear that Asim couldn't hear. The man turned back to the boy and said, "No Muslim should strike another Muslim, no brother should battle a brother. He was wrong. You needn't bow, but don't mock an elder, *ever*."

Asim didn't say anything. He was thinking of hitting his brother. *Maybe he'd leave me alone then,* he thought.

Tarik turned and walked into the office.

"He seems like a smart boy," the imam said to Ferran.

He turned to Asim: "Your brother said you're going to the University of Michigan. I know good Muslim men in Ann Arbor, brothers at the university. I could help you make friends. We have money, too, that could make things a little easier. All you have to do is a favor or two. A test of your loyalty."

Asim was surprised they knew about Michigan. "I don't need anyone's help," he said.

Tarik returned with the airline ticket peeking up from his shirt pocket.

"Let's wait in the car and let these brothers handle things on their own," the imam said, smiling. They walked out.

"I've never seen him smile. Consider yourself lucky," Tarik said when they'd gone.

"Why did you tell them about Michigan? I don't want anything to do with those assholes. I've told you, I don't want any part of this religious shit. Besides, I might stay here."

Tarik scowled. "Allah has no patience for your kind. Father burns because of his abominations. You had a chance, *faggot*."

Asim turned then, and kicked his brother in the groin. He was wearing thick Timberlands and Tarik doubled over.

Ferran, who had seen everything, ran back in and restrained Tarik.

"Stop," he told Tarik. "Do you want the police to pull up with the imam here? Remember, brother, a crucial rule: in a hostile place do not call attention to yourself. Be patient."

Asim was shaking. He had never hit his brother before.

"We hoped you would do us a favor. Your reward would be with Allah. But it looks like you aren't willing. Too bad, I think the imam likes you," Ferran said.

"He's—" Tarik said, and left it there, though Asim knew his brother wanted to say *fag*.

"Did you tell your brother you're leaving this afternoon for Islamabad, and then to religious training in the desert? He should know. Brothers should never leave each other in violence. A brother can be saved," Ferran said.

Tarik said, "Leave him."

"Tell him about *Tablighi Jamaat*," Ferran said.

"He's not interested."

"Every Muslim boy should know about the way to peace."

"You don't understand, he's like our father, an abomination. It's too late for Asim. He's even hanging around the Russian bitch."

Ferran looked confused and asked, "Who?"

"Never mind. Let's go," Tarik said.

Ferran grabbed Asim's hands, clasped them together and then pulled them apart just as suddenly. It was a weird ritual thing.

"There, now his faith is broken. He must earn it back," Ferran said.

Asim, unnerved, retreated to the inner lobby door; he just wanted them to leave. He said, "You're both fuckin' nuts."

Asim saw the look on his brother's face and could tell that Tarik could have easily killed him.

Asim thought, *Fuck you. Fuck all of you.*

He was about to go into the office when he heard the imam call his name. They met at the concession stand.

"You will be prudent and take this package to a Muslim brother at a mosque in Toronto. It's next to a bowling alley, Lucky Strikes. The address is here," he said, handing him a card.

"I won't take anything."

"Don't make up your mind so hastily," Shamal said. "I'm told you love the movies. You wouldn't want this place to explode. You don't want anything to happen to you or your sister."

He paused and waited for the boy to react, but Asim was too surprised to say anything. The boy's silence encouraged the imam.

"With a little religious training, I think you might see things differently," he said. "You could do great things for us at Michigan."

"I know a man in the FBI," Asim said, surprised that the lie came to him so easily.

"I know a thousand men who could slice your throat tomorrow morning, Allah willing. I know a believer in your FBI; he was skeptical in the beginning too. You will do this, or not. It's your decision. The consequences are yours."

The imam's matter-of-factness terrified him more than any of Tarik's threats. He managed to say, "Get out."

The imam ignored him and handed over a bunch of bills. "Your brother took everything. You will need the petty cash. You see, I know how American business works."

He turned to leave, but at the door, he paused.

"It is true. Allah says a Muslim must not commit violence against another Muslim. But there is an exception. About a brother who betrays a brother, the Koran says, *strike off his head and every fingertip.*"

Asim was silent.

"Someday you will see. Every Muslim must come to *jihad*. Be proud of your brother. Becoming a warrior isn't easy."

The white-robed stranger pointed to the package on the candy counter.

"Inside is a videotape about the great fruit of our struggle in Yemen. Do you like war movies? *Bridge over the River Kwai. Patton.* You see, I know a lot about American cinema. This tape's a trailer about *our* war, a hint of things to come. Our beloved sheik speaks in the video. Watch it before you take it to Toronto."

He paused, waited for a response, and when it was clear Asim was going to remain silent, he said, "Make Allah happy, boy."

The imam turned and left. A lake wind whined when the lobby door opened and snow from the squall blew in.

ALLAH'S REVENGE

FERRAN AND SHAMAL waited in the driveway while Tarik packed a duffel: white boxers, socks, a pair of jeans, T-shirts, a couple more turtlenecks. He didn't own a single piece of proper Muslim dress. He retrieved his toothbrush and paste. Back in his room, he looked around and wondered whether he should take a memento, but there was nothing he wanted. He thought, *Why not wipe out everything.* He didn't discard the doodle of the bowling ball bomb or the names of the hopeless Arabs in America. He was glad Asim would find them. He remembered the note about *towelheads* that had been posted on the Bethlehem door. He stuffed it into the bottom of the bag. *They'll see,* he thought. In the drawer, he found a still of Travis Bickle and placed it on the bed. DeNiro, shirtless, has a gun harness around his neck; a nickel-plated .38 in a holster is tucked under his armpit. On his other shoulder another black holster for a magnum .44 hangs the length of his torso. Behind him on a table are vials of pills. *Bennies,* Tarik remembered. He stared at DeNiro and recited Travis's lines: "*The idea had been growing in my brain for some time. True force. All the king's men cannot put it back together again . . . Here is a man who couldn't take it anymore.*" Maybe there was nothing on earth he loved more than *Taxi Driver.* He stuffed the photograph into the bottom of his bag. "Movie idolatry," the imam had told him, "It's forbidden." *I'm not perfect,* he thought.

He entered Masika's room, picked up an eye-liner pencil from the bureau, and wrote on the mirror in a small, careful script: *Far from easy for those without faith. Allahu akbar.* He knew he sounded preachy and was glad he'd come to this seriousness while everyone else wastes life on pleasures. He thought, *I've left her with a way to save herself. Allah believes in mercy.*

He walked into Asim's room and wrote with the makeup pencil, this time scrawling across his brother's mirror: *Soon Allah will visit with a mount of calamities.* He wasn't going to forget the humiliation of being kicked in front of Ferran. He wasn't going to forget his faggot brother.

To make a point he repeated the last sentence in Arabic, even though he knew his brother wouldn't know what it meant, and he added: *Someday a real rain will come.* His brother *would* recognize Travis Bickle. On his way out he forced himself to refrain from spitting on the bed where he'd heard Asim masturbate. He had heard everything and was sickened that his brother turned out so much like their father.

He remembered the Koran and fetched it from a drawer and put it into the sack; he wondered where he would be without it to guide him: *those of the left hand, how wretched are those of the left hand.* Except for his mother, the family was unholy. He paused, faced east, and asked for Allah's forgiveness for being born into this house.

He thought, *The Koran says take not from among the unbelievers a friend or a helper.* He knew his brother wouldn't come through for the imam.

He stopped by the door of his parents' room. His mother had already stripped it of every trace of his father: Shoe stretchers in a corner looked like a pile of prosthetic feet; his father's bureau was cleared of fancy colognes—Havana, Versace aftershave, Intuition, Fahrenheit, Tiffany Sport. His mother had filled fifteen trash bags with his father's clothes: Brooks Brothers shirts, Italian silk ties, even ascots; two drawers with boxers so bright and flashy she refused to touch them. As she had removed suits from hangers a pocket watch had fallen out. Engraved on the back: *to Badru from Sonia and Nicky.* She had thrown it against the wall. Before Tarik carted everything to the dump, he had said, "Mother, I'd burn it all if there was a safe place."

She didn't say anything.

For as long as he could remember he knew his father stayed out all night after the last movie. He had seen them walking in South Park. Who in Lackawanna hadn't? All the while his mother ended her day chanting Arabic. Women, he understood, were intended to be isolated. A believer didn't need a woman for satisfaction. His mother's isolation wasn't his father's fault. It was fucking the Russian; *that* was unclean. And the bitch's husband? Fucking him? *That* was unforgivable, an abomination. Sonia's shaking was Allah's revenge.

Once he had asked his father what the old man was doing with the old whore, and his father slammed him into the wall and said, "I'm tired of you judging me. Who do you think you are, Mohammed?"

Tarik had decided long ago he had to do something to redeem his name and please Allah. At first, he imagined dousing the theater seats with gasoline and watching outside the Bethlehem while flames consumed the movie house.

Then one night on CNN he saw a better way. It had happened in a Jerusalem pizzeria. A young man sat at a table with his guitar case between his legs and moments later a bomb blasted diners into pieces. He didn't see the explosion on TV, but he could picture the martyrdom. Men in yellow vests with plastic gloves and plastic bags tied over their shoes arrived on scooters. They picked through rubble for body parts and scraped flesh from walls. He imagined that someday instead of burning the theater he would pack a belt of a young martyr with explosives, ball bearings, and nails, and he would drive the boy to the theater, and from a distance, without anyone noticing, watch Asim sell the bomber a ticket. Sometime, not long after the lights had gone out, he would hear the explosion. Maybe Sonia would be sitting near the martyr and shrapnel would slice into her neck and brain, blind her before she bled out. This picture filled Tarik's heart with the peace that comes from serving God. He would make Asim sorry for befriending her.

He heard the horn outside and checked the plane ticket in his pocket. His flight had been booked for April—had Ferran made a mistake? Tarik picked up his bags and rushed out to the driveway.

"You ready, brother?" Ferran said.

"Yes, but my ticket's for a flight in April."

"We can exchange it in Newark. Things are moving faster than anyone expected."

Tarik didn't know what that meant and decided not to ask. He sat in the front. Before Ferran started the engine he said, "God is great."

Shamal sat silent in the back. Tarik wanted to turn and greet the imam and find a way to apologize for Asim, but Ferran whispered, "Leave him to himself. He said he wanted peace. What took you so long?"

He didn't answer right away, and then asked, "Will we meet any suicide bombers in Pakistan?"

Ferran gave him a look and said, "Sure."

"I've watched on television how a single *shahid* makes Israelis jittery for months."

Shamal leaned forward and said, "Patience," in a voice that sounded to Tarik like a slight rebuke.

The squall had exhausted itself and left behind flurries. In the rusted Volvo, bits of road ice and the cold blew in through holes in the floor; with nothing more than the imam's suitcase and a duffel bag each, they drove down the streets of Lackawanna. They passed Father Nelsen Baker's Home for Boys, Our Lady of Victory Basilica, the Yemen Soccer Field, the Ukrainian church transformed into the city's mosque. Tarik was glad to leave it all: the Italian bak-

ery with the stupid bride-and-groom-topped cakes, the Polish
meat market with links of sausages dangling from the ceiling, yellow happy-faces in the elementary school windows, statues of the
Virgin Mary tucked into front gardens. He had enough of their
idolatry. He had enough of Lackawanna. They passed the DB
Mart on Knowlton, run by a Yemeni who had sold out to America, and across the street Sonia's apartment and the firefighters
pulling in hoses and getting ready to return to the station. Tarik
smiled.

"Stop," Shamal said.

The imam opened his window and breathed in the sooty air. The
house was standing but the entire exterior of the third floor was
scorched.

"I watched this morning when a woman there was wheeled away
on a stretcher," the imam said. "I'd seen her earlier last night, before arriving at the mosque. She was on the bus—an old woman
who thought she was some Bollywood star. In Afghanistan, she
would have been stoned."

A yellow Labrador jumped up on the door and barked at Shamal.

"Get over here, Gabriel," someone called out.

Shamal scowled, and said, "Dogs here are always interested in
me."

Tarik had to force himself to hide his nervousness, and thought,
Why did Allah let her survive?

Ferran drove on Martin Street to the intersection of Ridge and
Abbott where he stopped at the light, and Tarik caught a last
glimpse of the Bethlehem's marquee and saw his brother's Cadil-

lac still outside the theater. He felt an unexpected and cavernous despair, and he thought, *No warrior should feel this way.* By the time the light changed and they moved on, the Bethlehem retreated out of sight. Within seconds the Volvo was on the thruway ramp and Tarik knew he would never see home again.

DUMDY-DOO-WAH

IN THE COLD AND NEARLY blackened theater, Asim sat close to the screen. The exit signs cast a reddish glare in the corners by the emergency doors. He kept his eyes on the one at the left, the letters wavering over a nervous fluorescent. He tried to figure out what was happening. He had left the package on the concession stand, and the wad of bills was still folded in his palm, which he hadn't opened since Shamal had pushed the money into his hand. He wished he really did know someone from the FBI, and wondered whether he should call the police anyway. He knew there was a Yemeni cop in the city, the only Arab on the force. Maybe the guy could help.

The outline of the movie screen sharpened while his eyes adjusted to the dark: it was gray, like a giant Etch-a-Sketch. He knew he should have been doing something about Tarik instead of hiding in a movie seat the way he'd always done when he wanted to escape whatever he couldn't stand. He used to sit alone in the theater when a movie wasn't playing and imagined turning knobs in the air until fidgety lines curled and looped into figures of movie characters. His favorite was the silhouette of Alfred Hitchcock: a bulging eggplant profile with thumbnail curves for eyes, a long apostrophe nose, two pinched fingertips for the mouth, and a shooting-star barrel chest. He'd seen *Psycho* and *The Birds* on his own and told his father they made him squeamish. "You have to learn to love Hitchcock," the old man said. Whenever a Hitchcock appeared on television, his father made sure they would see it, and sometimes he would order one and run it as a second feature. The old man loved to play the cameo game—"shout out when you see him and you win." His father's favorite was *Shadow of a Doubt*: "Seventeen minutes into the movie, you'll see him playing cards with a doctor on the train to Santa Rosa. Back to the camera, all eyes on Joseph Cotton, one of the scariest guys in the movies, ever." Asim set his watch to it, and sure enough, at seventeen minutes, the back of Hitchcock's head appeared, with hair then, not as fat, and a shoulder turned up as if he knew there was a reason to be tense. If you blinked, you missed him.

Now, Asim tried to etch the director onto the dark screen and couldn't. He wanted to imagine Travolta, but couldn't picture the sexy dancer. He took a stab at sad and creepy Johnny Depp in *Edward Scissorhands* with makeshift appendages of razors and shears.

Nothing emerged. He couldn't even trace beautiful Omar from the launderette. All he could envision was kicking his brother and the stranger's warning: "You don't want anything to happen to you and your sister." He thought, *Even if I go to Michigan, I'd be afraid they'd fuck up everything. Why didn't Tarik leave me out of this?*

He left the seat, picked up the package, and went into the office. He counted the money in his hand: two-hundred and fifty dollars. He decided he would go to Deaconess for Masika. He would bring her straight back and they would figure out what to do. He removed the video and wondered whether he should wait. He wondered whether this was a trick, some crazy test: He considered throwing the package in the Dumpster. He would never hear another thing about it. They wouldn't punish him. He fished around inside and found a stack of bills—fives, tens, twenties—wound tight with string. It could have been a thousand dollars, more. *Fuck,* he thought, *they're not going to forget about this much money.* There was a note: "Brother Salid, here are the victory tape and money for your wedding plans." The video was labeled "Attack on U.S.S. Cole." He removed it from its sleeve and slipped it into a portable player on the filing cabinet behind him.

The tape began with the sound of bomb blasts and rifle shots and across a black screen a line appeared: *Al-Sahab Productions.* A man appeared, dressed in a white robe and headscarf: tall, wiry, with a long dark beard that became scragglier as it draped down his neck. A dagger hung from a belt around his waist. He recited something in Arabic while the camera caught a fiery explosion on a ship with a subtitle: Destruction of the American Destroyer Cole.

Shit, Asim thought.

He watched scenes of Muslims being killed in Palestine, Chechnya, and Lebanon. The same robed guy they called the Tall One reappeared outside a cave, cradling a Kalashnikov. Footage of masked men traveling through a rugged desert waving black flags, and jumping hurdles and setting out explosives. Soldiers with Kalashnikovs—the word *MUHAJADEEN* flashing across the bottom of the screen—shot at images of Bill Clinton and King Hussein. Asim wondered whether he should take the tape to the police. Tarik was crazier than he thought, but Asim didn't want to cause *that* kind of trouble for his brother. There was no way he would deliver this package to a makeshift mosque next to a bowling alley in Toronto. His sister had to see this, he thought.

He returned the video to its sleeve. He stuffed it and the money back into the package. He opened the bottom drawer of the filing cabinet and dropped it in.

Someone knocked. He pushed in the drawer so hard it popped back out a few inches.

He thought, *How fucked am I?*

"Who's that?" he asked.

"Billy Maguire. I saw your Cadillac outside."

Asim opened the door. "How did you get in?"

"Lobby door was wide open. Snow was blowin' in."

"I've got to go pick up my sister." Asim fidgeted with his watch strap.

"Always in a hurry. I think you're afraid of me, kid." Billy smiled. "Don't know why. Just 'cause I'm Irish, I guess."

"I like Irish guys," Asim said. He thought, *What am I doing? Now, after what Tarik has left me with.* But he backed away and Billy came inside.

Billy was right. He was afraid. Tarik, the imam, masked men in a desert, loneliness, even Sonia—everything terrified him. Maybe Billy most of all. Maybe *that* was why he let the redhead in. Billy was the fear he could face.

"That woman isn't around?" Billy asked.

"Who?"

"The one who shakes."

"Sonia."

"She doesn't like me."

"She's got Parkinson's, and I think her memory's going. She was my father's—" He paused a second and said, "—friend. Funny, I think she was a little jealous." Talking to Billy like this, a little like a date, began to feel like a relief.

"She should be," Billy said, with a mock belligerence. He pointed to a poster of *Casablanca,* and said, "I love that." Bogart and Bergman were cheek to cheek, their faces blown up, covering three quarters of the poster, the sides of their lips nearly touching.

"My father had something for Bogart," Asim said, surprised he was telling Billy this.

"Really. He wasn't like in love with Bergman?"

"Maybe, but he liked Bogart more." He saw part of the package in the drawer was visible and hoped Billy wouldn't notice. He wished he knew the redhead well enough to tell him about Tarik.

Billy smiled. "You Arabs are mysterious." He sat on the desk, and said, "I love the scene where Bogart is alone at the table in a white jacket and black bow tie, kind of like a tuxedo. I can't remember what he's drinking but there's a half-empty bottle before him. He's got serious hound eyes, dark skin, hairy wrists. Kind of like a worn-out older version of you."

"I don't look anything like Bogart," Asim said.

"You do, but prettier."

Asim looked up at the poster.

Billy walked closer and cupped his hand on the back of Asim's head, leaned in, and kissed him. Asim felt warm breath filtering through his hair.

"Shh," Billy whispered. "Don't say anything." He took Asim's hand and held it against the front of his pants.

"See what you do to me, kid."

Asim kissed Billy's neck, the soft, pea-size glands under his jawbone, while he opened his zipper and guided Asim's hand into the slit.

Asim had a choice: He could break off now and get his sister and figure out what to do about Tarik, or he could stay with Billy and do what he'd been fearing for a long time.

He said, "*Only the Lonely,* that got my attention."

"I guess I'm resourceful when I decide on something," Billy said. He sang, almost in a whisper, "Dum-dum-dum-dumdy-doo-wah."

Asim laughed.

Then he pictured his brother and thought, *Fuck Tarik.*

Asim said, "I want to suck you."

"I thought I'd have you first." Billy paused, and then said, "It's your show, but let's make this a little more romantic."

He took off his parka and a thick fisherman's sweater, which Asim thought smelled sexy. He paused when he noticed Asim looking at his ribbed T-shirt, slipped it off, and said, "Come here. Put your arms around my waist."

Then he just said Asim's name.

It was the first time he had heard Billy say it, and the sound of it made him forget everything. Billy unbuttoned Asim's pants and pulled them down. He was wearing a pair of snowflake boxers.

Billy laughed. "Seasonal wear?"

He pulled them down too and knelt, but Asim stopped him. "You forgot. I said I wanted you."

Asim remembered the video, and thought, *How can I be doing this now?* But he didn't want to stop.

Billy placed a hand on his head and drew him in, until the smell of sex was all that mattered. Asim took Billy inside and was amazed that he could make this man breathe so hard. The beautiful redhead sighed and spilled into him, warm and milky, even more mysterious than Asim had imagined.

When it was over, Billy dropped to his knees and said, "Louis, I think this is the beginning of a beautiful friendship."

Asim said, "I'm glad you like the movies."

"I like you."

"I've never tasted anyone before."

Billy raised his brows and smiled. "That's beautiful."

"What?"

"A first time."

Asim didn't say anything. He remembered Tarik and everything else and wanted to run.

Billy kissed him and said, "Your turn."

"I can't."

Asim knew he was spoiling everything, and thought, *I'll confide in him. I'll show him the video. I'll tell him about the Egyptian Queen Boat.*

"Don't get freaky, kid. This isn't just a trick in the park. You could tell, right? That was a real kiss." He sounded nervous.

Billy dressed, and sang, "You must remember this / A kiss *isn't* just a kiss / A sigh *isn't* just a sigh."

"See, I mean it," he said. "I've been watching you so long from the Pig Iron that I think you've driven me a little batty."

"Maybe we can meet tonight, after the show." Asim thought, *Later I'll tell him everything.*

"Okay." Billy sounded as if he wasn't sure Asim had meant it.

"I've got a lot to think about," Asim said.

"I've got a lot of convincing to do," Billy said.

Billy paused, and said, "I'm leaving, kid. I'm leaving happier than I've ever been. I think you're beautiful."

Asim took his hand.

"Killer smile," Billy said.

"Do you like *Zhivago?*"

"It's schmaltzy, but not so bad."

"*A good love gone bad*. Is that your song?"

"Yeah, but I don't believe that's what always happens."

"I see."

"You see a lot for a kid."

"You're not afraid of Arabs?"

"That's a stupid question. I'm not afraid of much."

"You drink a lot."

"I'm Irish."

Asim was quiet for a while and said, "I like your red hair." *What am I doing?* he thought.

Billy kissed him again, and walked out.

Asim pulled up his pants and found his shirt on the chair. He sat for a minute, thinking about Billy. He noticed the package again; when he was on his knees, Billy must have reared back and jarred the drawer open even more. *Masika*, he remembered. Maybe she'd know what to do. He cleared a spot in the back of the safe and took the package from the cabinet and jammed it as far back into the safe as it would go.

He thought, *Fuck Tarik*.

GABRIEL SNIFFING

IN THE CAR ASIM couldn't concentrate. His mind was strobo-scopic, flashing back to Billy, the menacing imam, Tarik glaring at him naked on his way to the shower. He pictured his father and Sonia and tried to imagine Nicholas. He saw shirtless men dancing on the Queen Boat on the Nile and then the barracks where other men in white coats with scalpels in their hands were waiting. He got hard remembering Billy.

Passing the Yemen Soccer Field he had almost forgotten that So-nia lived across the street until he noticed a fire truck, the last one that had stayed for the cleanup. He saw that the clapboards of her third-floor apartment were blistered and blackened, pulled over, braking suddenly. The fire truck was heading out.

He didn't recognize anyone, but approached a man in a parka with a clipboard, and thinking the guy was a reporter, he asked, "The woman who lives there, is she okay?" His voice was shaky. He thought, *What else can happen today?*

He remembered what Tarik had once said about Sonia, "I'll make that bitch pay."

"Who are you?" the man asked.

"A friend," he said.

Gabriel wandered over and sniffed at his thigh. Gordon followed.

"What kind of friend?"

Asim sensed the man wasn't a reporter and then saw "Erie County Fire Marshal" on the clipboard cover.

"I own the theater. She goes to see a movie every week. Last night I dropped her off."

"You're young to own a theater," the guy said.

Gordon broke in. "They took her to Deaconess. She wasn't hurt too bad, coughed a lot, but I don't think she needed a stretcher. EMTs always overreact. Gabriel smelled the smoke before anyone. I called it in."

"You live here too?" the fire marshal asked. "Why didn't anybody tell me you live here?"

Gordon said, "You didn't ask."

Gabriel jumped up on Asim's leg and licked his hand where he had wiped Billy's cum from his lips. Asim, embarrassed, pulled his hand away.

"He's friendly, loves everyone. Gabriel's the first thing Sonia saw when she unlocked the door. I think he knows he did something pretty good."

Asim didn't say anything and walked back to the car.

"Nice car," Gordon shouted. "I like an old Cadillac. Can I hitch a ride?"

Asim paused and turned around. "Where're you going?"

"Nowhere special. I just like riding in a Cadillac."

"I want to get to the hospital. Maybe some other day." For a moment he wondered whether the guy was coming on to him.

"Hey, where are you going?" the fire marshal asked. "If you know the old lady who lives here, I've got some questions for you, kid."

Asim turned to continue back to the car. He thought, *Why is everyone calling me "kid"*? "I'll be at Deaconess, if you want to talk."

He thought, *At least Sonia is okay.*

FIDDLE-DEE-DEE

SONIA REMEMBERED that Nicholas had sad eyes, black and contemplative, like the eyes in the icon of the Vladimir Mother. When she saw them for the first time, in the foyer the night her father had brought him home, she knew loving him wasn't going to be easy. Even at seventeen, she knew. In high school, she had more boyfriends than she could count, and then, when she saw Nicky, none of them mattered.

Her father once told her, "You look like Jean Harlow. You better watch out—you don't want boys to think you're a tart."

She didn't know who Jean Harlow was until she was thirty and the Bethlehem showed *The Beast of the City* in a gangster movie revival weekend. She was surprised because she really did look a little like the blond bombshell. She loved it when the actress walked into the speakeasy in a low-necked dress and shiny black hat that showed off her blinding hair. Harlow didn't need diamonds to look great.

But Nicky had seen right away that Sonia was more than blond and pretty. She didn't know what she was getting into, but she knew, with Nicky, it wouldn't be easy.

"Sonia," Masika said. "You look kind of dreamy."

"I was thinking about a boy."

Masika laughed. "I bet you were."

"You're pretty as Asim," she said.

"I called him, but he isn't home or at the theater. I know he'll come to see you."

He's probably with the scarlethead, she considered saying but knew she shouldn't start any trouble.

Instead, "You should have a boyfriend," she said.

"Who says I don't?"

Sonia remembered the doctor who winked at Masika and said, "You ain't so tough."

"What's that mean? You're not making much sense. You still have smoke on the brain?"

Sonia smiled. "I was thinking about one of Jean Harlow's gangsters. He should have stayed home with her instead of packing it in on a rainy street with the nobodies around to hear him say, *I ain't so tough.*"

In a voice so low that Masika couldn't hear, she added, "Nicky was restless too."

"Father told me no one loved the movies like you."

"You didn't know Nicky."

"I know more than you think."

"He was tortured." Her shaking intensified.

"Don't think about it now."

"They said Nicky was crazy. He wasn't crazy. He knew what he was doing. He made everyone else suffer. I tried to help him but he wouldn't let me. He wouldn't let your father help. Sometimes I talk to him as if he were alive. I tell him, 'you're a selfish bastard.'"

She took shallow breaths and her hands trembled under the hospital sheet.

Masika tried to change the subject. "So when did you meet Asim?"

Sonia heard but didn't want to talk about the boy. She thought, *he's not interested in me.*

She said, "You're a saint."

Masika laughed. "Right."

"You're not selfish like me."

"I don't think you're selfish."

"You don't know. You're the saint, it runs in the family."

"I'm not religious. And Tarik, he's no saint."

"Don't talk about him."

"The sedative should calm you soon."

Sonia said, "Fiddle-dee-dee."

When Masika didn't answer, she said, "Your father loved to play name-the-movie-line. Nicky used to play too, until one day he just said it bored him. That was when the worst of it began."

"'Fasten your seat belts, it's going to be a bumpy night,'" Masika said.

Sonia smiled and said, "You can play too? Badru adored Betty Davis. That was a good one."

Sonia thought and said, "'Have another martini.'"

Masika laughed.

"'A census taker once tried to test me. I ate his liver with some fava beans and a nice Chianti.'" Sonia winked.

"You can quote Lector. I'm shocked. 'Old age, it's the only disease that you don't look forward to being cured of,'" Masika said.

"Your father was the only person in the world who thought Orson Welles was handsome. He liked soulful actors. 'This is one nutty hospital.'"

"'We all go a little mad sometimes . . . haven't you?'" Masika asked.

"He loved Hitchcock more than anyone. He stumped us all of the time."

She paused and said, "'It's midnight. One half of Paris is making love to the other half.'"

"Damn, I don't know that one," Masika said.

"Too bad, that's Garbo. The old lady in the hospital gown wins."

Masika squeezed her arm and whispered, "I'm glad my father loved you."

"You know nothing, honey." Sonia brought Masika's hand to her lips and kissed it. "I miss him as much as Nicky, maybe more."

Masika turned and saw Asim. He had been standing in the doorway long enough to hear the last part of the game. Sonia had not noticed until he walked over to the bed and patted her shoulder.

"The protector," she said.

He smiled. "Looks like you need protecting."

"A dog saved me."

"I met him."

The sedative was kicking in. The last thing she heard was Masika, trailing off: "We'll be here when you wake up. You're coming home with us."

DAY-GLO

ASIM WAITED FOR Masika as she wheeled Sonia from the ER to a hospital room. In the waiting lounge, he sat across from a family. The mother wasn't Arab, but she wore a white head scarf so that all he could see were her bright blue eyes, sandstone cheeks, a snub nose, slightly misaligned mouth. He wondered whether her face was oval, square, or shaped like a pear. Under the scarf it was impossible to tell. Asim sensed that she didn't want to be dressed in Muslim clothes. She cradled a baby. A boy, maybe six or seven, stared at him. The kid was wearing a Spiderman T-shirt under a Day-Glo yellow down parka. He held a GameBoy, but was more interested in Asim. The father had a dish towel, stained with blood, wrapped around a hand. He nodded at Asim as if they knew each other.

The guy got up, crossed the room, and sat next to him. "Sliced my palm on a can of tuna. Nurse wants a doctor to sew it up."

Asim nodded. The guy's wife looked over. The kid smiled.

"You're Tarik's brother."

The side of Asim's neck pulsated. He nodded.

"I was with him last night at the mosque. He's pretty opinionated."

"That's him."

"He's real serious about Islam. I admire that."

Asim didn't say anything.

The man's voice dropped to a whisper. "You know about the pilgrimage in April? A bunch of us are going to Pakistan to learn about becoming better Muslims. My wife doesn't know."

Asim gave him a look and said, loud enough for the guy's wife and kid to hear, "I don't give a shit about any of this Islam crap."

The guy, surprised, got up and went back to sit next to his wife, who looked like she had to catch herself from smiling. The boy got up and ran to his father.

Masika returned. "The doctor is keeping her for the night. He wants to make sure her lungs are clear. He told me he also wants to be sure she isn't a psych case."

Asim, seeing that the guy with the bloodied hand was listening, didn't say anything.

"She'd been asking for you. I didn't know you've spoken much with her," Masika said.

"She started coming to the movies again. I've taken her home a couple of times. She's a little wacky, but I like her. She's not crazy."

Masika said, "I should have asked you before I said anything about taking her in for a while. She's alone. I think Father would have wanted us to help out."

"I'm glad you did. About a year ago, he asked me to take care of her if anything happened to him."

"He talked to me too."

Asim remembered the tape, and whispered, "Can you get out of here? It's about Tarik. It's bad."

"What?"

He looked at the guy again, and whispered, "I don't want to talk about it here."

Masika looked across the room too, and seemed to understand. "I'm done for the night. I'll tell Sonia we'll see her tomorrow," she said.

His sister came right back and said, "She's out like a light."

Inside the car, on the way to the theater, Asim became suddenly hesitant about telling her what was going on with Tarik. Instead, he kept on Sonia.

"I didn't expect to like her."

"You know that she loved Father."

"I know everything," he said. "When I was five, I saw them naked."

"Where?"

"Upstairs, in the room next to the projection booth."

"You're kidding."

"Why would I make this up?"

"Did Father know?"

"Sure."

"Who could blame him?" Masika asked. "I'm glad he loved someone."

Asim didn't hear, and as they neared the street where they lived, he said, "You know, Tarik's crazier than we knew. We had a fight. You won't believe what he left me."

"*God*, I didn't think of this. They can't be in the house together. I wish he were going to Pakistan now instead of April."

He was about to tell her that Tarik had already left with Ferran and the imam—and everything else—but she touched his arm and burst out with, "Wait, let's stop at home a minute. I'm going to change."

"Can't you do that later?"

"I smell of disinfectant."

In the driveway, she said, "If Tarik's home, I'll tell him he has to leave. I don't want him around. The neighbors have called the cops enough times. He's unpredictable. I'm sick of it. If he doesn't leave, I'll tell the cops he hits me."

Asim was surprised by the depth of her disdain.

She paused and said, "He slapped me once. That's enough. He's out, and Sonia's coming home with us."

"Masika—" he said. But she had already left the car before he could tell her that Tarik had already gone.

He thought, *I wish I knew the end to this.*

Then he surprised himself by picturing Billy. He smiled, and thought, *Masika is going to like him. Sonia will have to get used to him*. But he pictured his brother, too, holding a Kalashnikov and shooting at pictures of George Bush in the desert.

He shook his head, and thought, *I've got to get out of Lacka-wanna*.

Masika shouted to him from the house, "Asim, come in, *now*."

At the door, she grabbed his arm and dragged him upstairs, where he read Tarik's messages scrawled across the mirrors.

"What's happening?" Masika asked.

"Wait until you see the video."

Wednesday, September 5, 2001
GHOST WORLD

ASIM HAD BARELY slept, and though he didn't want to re-turn to the theater, with the skull waiting in the safe, he did—early—to change the marquee. It was the week to show a film few movie houses offered—the first indie he had selected. For a moment the anticipation of the new film almost made him forget about Tarik. When his father used to pick an indie, it was usually something hard to figure out, a movie like *Memento*, something that would keep an audience guessing. His first selection was lighter, and he wondered what his father would have thought of it: *Ghost World*.

He liked the poster: two girls, outcasts, one in black work boots and black socks pulled halfway up her calves, obviously in charge, with a black and neon green skirt, a Raptor T-shirt, thick black-rimmed glasses, straight dark hair, while the other, glomming on to her—a gangling blonde who was on the verge of becoming beautiful. In the corner of the poster was a still of an older guy, an obvious loser—Steve Buscemi—waving a Jimmy Reed vinyl. Asim thought that Buscemi had stolen the show in *Fargo*. In the *Ghost World* poster, over the actor's head in a cartoon thought-bubble was the line: *Is it just me, or did we have a moment?* The movie had to be good. He wondered whether the two girls and Buscemi were doing a kind of *The Graduate* thing.

When Sonia saw the coming attractions the week before, she had said, "I don't think I'm going to like this."

He told her she might be surprised.

"Those girls look like they hate everything. Maybe it's better you like boys," she said.

With a pail of marquee letters in one hand and a hook pole in the other, he went outside and thought, *What am I going to do about Tarik? Christ, the fucking skull he left me yesterday.* All night he had replayed in his mind his brother's voice on the tape calling him a *dirty faggot.* If his brother was in trouble because Asim hadn't delivered the video and money for the imam, he didn't care. He never wanted any part of Tarik's shit. His mind hadn't changed. *What kind of brother drops off a skull?* he thought.

He should have told Masika, but he knew her response would have been the same as what she had said about the video from the desert: "Call the cops." Tarik probably had dropped off the skull himself. He remembered thinking he had seen his brother in the white van. Maybe Tarik was watching now. Maybe he knew that Sonia was living with them.

If Asim turned to the cops, he didn't know what his brother would do. What if they didn't arrest Tarik, only questioned him and let him go? He would know who had betrayed him. Asim wanted to think it all through. His head was pounding.

He was cleaning the billboard glass with an ammonia solution that made him gag. He hadn't noticed Billy sneaking up.

"Don't you love him? He's such an ugly bastard," Billy said. "He's got eyes like a Chihuahua." He kissed Asim, and said, "I don't get it. You're sexy even when you smell of ammonia."

"The whole street can see."

"Let 'em."

Asim didn't like open displays of affection. For months he worried the Muslim fanatics would see. He didn't want any trouble: broken windows, graffiti. Who knew what the bastards would do? And the men at the Pig Iron were not much better. Again he thought, *What if Tarik is watching?*

He knew he'd have to tell Billy about Tarik, but it was hard to be an open book like his father. Besides, he wasn't sure whether he really loved Billy.

He thought, *Billy could do a lot better. "Only The Lonely." I wonder if he understands how the song fits.*

The redhead was gushy. He had a temper. If Asim told him that Tarik was back—everything else—he might do something stupid.

"You're an idiot. Why aren't you working?" Asim said.

"Can't a guy take an afternoon off?"

Billy was the accountant at Father Baker's; sometimes he helped kids, not much younger than Asim, with math homework when they got back from sports practice. No one at Father Baker's knew he was gay; no one knew he drank a lot at the Pig Iron. Or if the priests knew, they pretended they didn't. Everyone thought he wasn't much different from other Irish guys who had grown up in Lackawanna. The only thing that made him stand out was his past—his parents. They had shot themselves while Billy was on his way home from a statistics class at Canisius. The day Billy told Asim about the suicides, he said that he wondered whether they had counted to three before they pulled the triggers. He confided that he wondered about their last thoughts, but doubted that they were about him. There was no note. Billy found his mother and father slumped over each other on the couch and called the priests before cops or rescue. Since then, he had lived at Father Baker's, first in a dormitory room, eventually in an apartment like a suite for a priest. Two rooms: one with a bed, bureau, a soft chair and television; the other with a kitchen table barely big enough for two. A hot plate and fridge. A crucifix in each room. The bathroom was down the hall. He called himself Father Baker's oldest orphan. More than once he had told Asim: "The fathers keep their compassion at arm's length."

"I thought I'd take the afternoon off and go to the park for old time's sake. Instead I ended up here," he said.

"Funny guy. You're lucky you never got caught in the bushes."

"I'm just lucky, period. What about that room upstairs? It's got a cot."

"You think you're *that* lucky."

They went into the office for the key.

"What's that?" Billy asked, pointing to the box sticking out of the safe.

Asim winced. "None of your business."

"You're always hiding stuff. What is it, cocaine bricks?" Billy shook his finger like a classroom priest.

"Cocaine comes in bricks?" Asim shoved the box back in. He noticed the Michigan catalogue, and covered it with an invoice.

"What about that cot?" Billy asked.

Asim, suddenly taken by the distraction, said, "Let's go."

He unlocked the room next to the projection booth and tightened a light bulb in the wall socket. *What if someone walks in?* he thought. He locked the door.

"Romantic. Lockdown, sort of like a prison cell," Billy said.

"I like this place. It's got a lot of history."

Billy looked bewildered but didn't say anything.

He had never told Billy about catching his father naked with Sonia. He couldn't think of anything intensely personal he had ever shared. He'd been sleeping with Billy a few times a week and all that this boyfriend really knew was that Asim liked movies; and yet he sensed he had discovered everything about Billy. He was even afraid to mention Michigan. He thought, *How can Billy believe he loves me? He doesn't know anything. What kind of lover keeps so many secrets?*

Asim touched Billy's thigh.

"For a kid, you know how to excite a guy," Billy said.

A kid, Asim thought. *See how little he knows.*

He looked around the room and pictured his father in bed with

Sonia's husband, and wondered how she could have loved two men at the same time. Wasn't it hard enough with one? He flashed back to Billy, and smiled. He had almost forgotten about the skull.

"You're pretty sexy for an old guy," he said, unbuckling Billy's belt. He pulled down the pants zipper. In private, he had remained the aggressor. He reached up and loosened the bulb and the room went dark. He wondered whether Nicky had joined his father and Sonia in this room. He wondered whether sex had obliterated everything for his father, and worried that it didn't for him. He thought, *Tarik's a lot sexier than me and look how he wastes it.* He wished he could forget about Tarik.

"Sweet today," Billy said.

Asim pulled Billy down to the cot.

"Can we just lie here a while?" he asked. "Hold me, with your arm around my side. Don't say anything."

"Whatever you want. Are you okay?"

Asim pretended to sleep.

Later, when the bells of Our Lady of Victory tolled, he envisioned Tarik prowling the city in the van.

"What's wrong? You're nervous." Billy said, screwing in the lightbulb.

"I've got to get the show ready. Tony's going to be here soon."

"Something's wrong."

"Nah."

Billy shook his head, as if he knew saying nothing was as good as saying something.

They dressed and walked outside. Asim thought, *I hope he doesn't try to kiss me.*

A black guy in jeans with a Kufi cap and thick beard was waiting at the doors.

"Are you Asim?"

"Why?"

He handed over an envelope. He stuttered. "You bet-bet-bet-better make sure you follow his orders. He's agitated."

"Who?" Billy asked.

"This isn't your bu-bu-business," the guy said.

"Fuck you. Why don't you take off that cap and go find Jesus, asshole."

"Don't, Billy." Asim took his arm, afraid he was going to hit the stranger, who mumbled something in Arabic, then walked off.

"What's going on?"

"It's my fuckin' brother. He's back." Asim was fingering the note.

"I thought he was in Pakistan, gone for good. What's *that* say?"

"Not now. Come back later, we'll talk about it."

"Maybe it can't wait until later," Billy said.

He reached for the note, but Asim stuffed it into a pocket.

Billy took his hand and pulled him in and whispered, "You've got to let me get closer."

"What if someone at the Pig Iron notices."

"I don't mean like that. Anyway, who the fuck cares who sees? And what's the big deal if Tarik's home?"

"You're right," Asim said.

Billy gave him a look, and said, "You're going to tell me everything."

"Later."

Asim didn't know what anyone could do.

Billy walked off, and once on the other side of the street, he turned and shouted, "Don't forget—later."

Asim waved and returned to the office. He sat and opened the note:

"Meet me Sunday in Niagara Falls on the last sail of the *Maid of the Mist*. Don't let your fag friend tag along. This is brother to brother. If you don't come I'll find that Russian bitch when she's alone. Then I'll hunt down that Irish faggot. Maybe I'll torch the house. Maybe I'll torch the orphanage. You got me into more trouble than you know, and now you've got to get me out. Bring the video and the money. That bitch's skull would make a good ash bowl."

Asim stared at the note, thinking he should have listened to Masika and told the cops about Tarik after the fire. *I'm always hoping things will go away,* he thought.

He picked up the Michigan catalogue and threw it in the trash. "Like that's going to ever happen," he said. Then he called the police station.

"I want to talk to the Yemeni cop," he said.

"Hamid?"

"If that's him."

"Who's this?" the dispatcher asked.

"A citizen."

"We don't like wise guys."

Asim hung up. What was he going to tell the cop anyway: *My brother's crazy. He sent me a skull.*

He took out the box and put the skull on the table. It wasn't an hallucination like he'd hoped. He wished Tarik had stayed in the desert and none of this was happening. He reached to call the Yemeni cop again and heard Tony carrying in canisters of film, and instead, he put everything back in the safe.

Tony gave him a look. "These the ones, Asim? *Ghost World?* You aren't going to make money from some weirdo high school chick flick. But, hey, I'm just the projectionist."

"It's for a couple of nights, Tony. On Friday, we're running *From Hell.*"

"Great. Never heard of it either." He paused and asked, "Kid, you okay?"

"I just woke up. I was upstairs sleeping."

"You never sleep."

"I went to the Pig Iron last night and got blasted."

"You never drink."

"That's why I was sleeping."

Tony shrugged. "*Ghost World.* It's because of movies like this that your father struggled."

Asim didn't answer.

Tony picked up the canisters and went upstairs.

Asim stuffed Tarik's note back into his pocket. *Okay,* he thought, *I'll meet you.*

It was almost 6:45. He had to go out front and sell tickets. About twenty showed for the seven o'clock, which wasn't bad considering it was a late summer evening when people were outside in the park or getting cones at Dairy Queen. Tony came down for a Coke and was surprised at the house.

"They only came for the air-conditioning," he said.

Five high school girls in the class behind Asim arrived together. They were all blondes, Polish probably, except for Lucy Perrilli. He used to catch her watching him, and sometimes she lingered until they were the only two left in a room or corridor. Last year, the semester before he graduated, they were in art together for two weeks, which he had to drop because a guidance counselor noticed he had missed physics. He had seen her here and there, but he'd thought she had lost interest, and he was surprised that he wished she hadn't.

"Asim," she said.

"Lucy, hi."

"I heard your father owned this place, but I've never seen you here."

"He died just before Christmas."

"I'm sorry."

He didn't answer.

"Lucy," one of the girls called. "We're going to get seats." They all waved at Asim like they knew him.

"I'll be right there," she said. She glanced around, and then lowered her voice. "You know my father's a cop, an FBI agent."

"FBI," he said. "You're joking, right?"

She motioned him closer. "I think your brother's in trouble. I overheard my dad talking about him on the phone. I think there's some list of Arabs they're checking out and your brother's on it. Later, he asked me about you. He remembered I used to mention you sometimes and he wanted to know what I thought about you."

"He's in Pakistan," Asim said, and thought, *Why am I lying to her, why am I telling her anything?*

"Good riddance. I met him once at the DB Mart. I bumped into him by mistake and he looked like he was going to smack me. He said something weird—that 'a woman shouldn't ever touch a man like that.' All I did was bump into him."

"I think he's trouble too."

"You're nothing like him. I'm going to tell my father I told you, okay?"

He didn't say anything.

"I think he's going to talk to you anyway."

"Why?"

"He's not a bad guy. I heard him say on the phone that a lot of Arabs in Lackawanna are getting a lousy rap. He's not a bigot. He's been on a cruise with Mom down the Nile. I told him I thought you were, well, sweet."

"A cruise down the Nile," he said. He decided he had to ditch her. He thought, *What the fuck is Tarik doing to me?*

"I've got to get the movie started."

"I like Thora Birch. She was pretty sexy in *American Beauty*."

He knew she was flirting, and he decided it wasn't a good idea to get close to her. He turned away, as if what she'd said hadn't registered.

He flipped off the house lights, and in the seconds before Tony started the movie he stood at the top of the aisle and looked back to see if there were stragglers looking for Raisinettes or popcorn. When he saw no one was waiting, he decided to sit for a while.

As the screen flashed with the first movie images, he was relieved—even with everything that was happening he thought he might be able to surrender to the spectacle. He could count on a movie, no matter how sad or happy it turned out. For a while, he thought, Tarik didn't matter, and maybe Billy would want to go to Ann Arbor, and maybe *that* would be okay. Maybe the skull was just a stupid threat and everything would end there. Sometimes when he was a kid he pretended he was the Italian village boy and his old man was the projectionist, Alfredo, in *Cinema Paradiso*. His father had told him that the first flickers of a movie had the power to transport you to a place where, for a while, your own fears and hardships didn't matter anymore. And when a movie ended, just before the lights flashed on, you could store a piece of whatever celluloid joy you might have found and save it for a time when it might do some good. Asim wished he had asked his father how to claim that kind of comfort. He wondered whether a movie even had this power. He remembered Tarik's note about their father: "movie house fool."

Asim was stunned by the musical bang, an Indian song-and-dance. This wasn't what he had expected, and he thought, *There's Arab shit everywhere, even in this movie about high school misfits.* It was the kind of music that would bring Bollywood moviegoers to their feet to dance in the aisles. He had read about those audiences. They shouted to actors on the screen, swooned, and threw things, and if they could, they would have leaped inside the films and joined the actors. He was relieved when the musical number ended and the movie switched to the bedroom of the restless girl from Los Angeles where every apartment building looked the same, where everyone was drinking cappuccino and shopping at 7-Eleven, everyone except this one dark-haired girl who looked like she belonged only to herself.

He thought, *I like her.*

He heard someone coughing at the concession stand.

"Gummy bears," said one of the blondes from school, who was waiting impatiently when he got to the counter. "This movie looks like it's going to suck."

"How do you know? It only just started."

"Arab crap," she said. "Oops, I didn't mean anything against you." She turned, not really embarrassed.

Asim went outside and stood on the sidewalk. He looked for the Bubble Wash van but couldn't see it. He watched the sun set blocks away, slinging itself over the dome of Our Lady of Victory. The sky was fiery—orange, pink, red.

"It's the filth from Buffalo," he remembered his old man had told him. "Isn't it stunning?"

He remembered saying, "Stunning, Dad?" He wasn't like his father. He couldn't see the beauty in everything.

He thought: *I'll meet him outside the* Maid of the Mist. *I'll return the tape and tell him I don't want anything to do with it, with any of his shit. I'll tell him he can keep the money. I'll warn him that if he tries to hurt Masika or Sonia, I'll make him pay. I'll say, "I know a girl whose father in the FBI is looking for bastards like you. I swear I'll turn you in." I'll tell him I don't give a fuck that he and Allah hate fags. I'll say, "Go fuck yourself, Tarik." I'll tell him I'm going to Michigan with my boyfriend. I won't get on the boat with him. I'll leave him standing there. Like that, it will be over.*

Or maybe I should go see Lucy's father.

THEY SHOOT HORSES, DON'T THEY?

*S*ONIA TOOK OUT the plate of chicken salad with grapes and walnuts that was left for her. She had an hour before the bus arrived. She had only put on lipstick and a little eye shadow. She would wear the cotton dress Masika had given her even though she thought it was dowdy—daisies on a pinkish background—barely a garment at all. She would need a sweater because by the second show the air-conditioning turned the Bethlehem into an icehouse. She ate her supper and put on the stupid dress. *The night is too sticky for rouge,* she thought. *Anyway, Asim doesn't care how I look. He's interested in the Irish guy. I'm tired of counting on men.* She had remembered to take every pill and was glad she wasn't shaking. *I'm* *not crazy,* she thought. It was dark enough when she walked outside that she saw fireflies blinking in the backyard. Nicky had called them the hit parade and said they lit up the night like high notes in a jazz café.

"That one over there," she remembered telling him, pointing to a blank section of the sky.

He said he couldn't see anything.

"It's 'bye-bye, blackbird'," she said, thinking about her mother. "My father only hit her when he was drunk," she told Nicky. "But he was drunk a lot."

"I know," he said.

He kissed her. This happened long before he had grown tired of everything. He said, "Tomorrow we'll go to Crystal Beach and ride the Comet."

The night he killed himself she was watching *They Shoot Horses, Don't They?* Badru had come to her seat and led her into the office. He had never interrupted a movie before; she knew something devastating had happened. He asked her to sit, and then he stood behind her and put his arms around her shoulders. He tried to kiss her neck and she flinched.

"What happened to Nicky?" she asked.

"He's dead."

He held her tighter when he said this as if he could contain her loss.

"Bastard," she said.

Badru was weeping.

When she reached the bus stop she was exhausted and thought,

Why can't I forget? She leaned against the lamppost and wished she could swing herself around it like Gene Kelly. She wished it were raining. It was so hot she thought she might faint. She slid herself down the post and leaned against the iron and felt something dig into her shoulder blade. The coarse concrete was like sandpaper on her thighs. The varicose blotches on her legs disgusted her. She felt something seep through her dress.

She remembered telling Badru, "If he loved anyone, he wouldn't have killed himself." He held her close and told her she was being harsh.

"What do you know about being harsh?" she said.

The bus pulled up and Johnny, the driver, rushed out and asked, "Sonia, what happened?"

"He's a bastard."

"Who?"

"Nicky."

"Did you fall?"

"He wasn't pushed. He crawled into the fire."

"What fire?"

"The blast furnace."

"I'm going to call for help."

"Just lift me up, Johnny." She was coming back to her senses. "I'm old and stupid."

He put a hand under her arm and lifted. She helped herself up and was surprised she wasn't shaking any more than usual.

"See, I'm fine. I don't want to miss the opener. You don't want to be late on the route."

"You sure you're okay?"

"It's hot. Can't a woman sit for a while waiting for a bus? You should have benches."

He smiled. "Okay, let's go. But I'm going to tell Asim how I found you."

She glared at him, and thought, *Go ahead, tell him. See if he cares.*

There were about a dozen riders on the bus, all women, mostly middle-aged, dressed in black skirts and white shirts. She didn't recognize anyone. She paid her fare, and while she walked to her spot in the back, she felt their stares. One of the younger women smiled as she passed.

"Hello," Sonia said. "Hot for this time of the evening in September, isn't it? You'd think Niagara Frontier could afford a little air conditioning."

The woman nodded.

She noticed Johnny in the huge surveillance mirror above the dash looking back and rolling his eyes, as if to say, "Your guess is as good as mine."

"Who are you all?" Sonia asked the woman, who handed her a pamphlet—"What Does God Require of Us?" Stamped in red on the back was Watchtower Publications, Jehovah Witnesses, Kingdom of God.

She turned a page and read the header—"Who is the Devil?" She looked at the woman, and handed it back.

"If you find him, kiss him for me," Sonia said.

The woman gave her a look.

She thought, *I look like hell.*

Once she was in her seat, the bus continued down Holland toward Ridge. Outside the window she pictured balloons shaped like bloated dolls floating along the road; the sidewalk was patched with balloon shadows luring girls and boys into a wood where houses and stores should have been. She used to be able to decide what movie she wanted to remember, but lately a movie had its own way with her, as *M* did then on the bus, out of nowhere. She closed her eyes and thought, *Not Peter Lorre, not tonight.* And when she opened them the bus had already stopped, Johnny was calling her, and outside the window was the Bethlehem.

"Funny," Johnny said. "He's always waiting for you."

She looked where Asim usually stood. "I'll be okay."

"What's the name of the film?"

"I don't like tests."

"The name, and don't look at the marquee, or I don't drive anywhere."

The women in black and white looked nervous.

"*Ghost World*," she said. "You should know I don't miss an opener."

"I'll wait until you're inside."

"I have always depended on the strangeness of kindness," she said, pausing to see if he would catch that she had botched Blanche Dubois, but all he did was nod. She looked back and saw him waving through the long narrow bus door window, lights from the marquee twinkling in the passenger windows as he pulled away.

Any minute the movie would start, and she was worried because Asim wasn't in the lobby. He wasn't behind the concession stand. She walked to the center aisle and tried to see how many moviegoers were in the house, but her eyes couldn't adjust. She walked back and opened the door to the office, looking up at the steep stairs to the projection booth. Asim was at his desk chair, hunched, and reaching inside the safe. She coughed.

When he heard her, he bolted upright.

"Sonia, oh Christ, I forgot."

"I know," she said, obviously hurt, hoping she would make him feel guilty, but he didn't seem to notice.

"'*Oh Christ*'? Why have you started saying that? Your father wouldn't approve."

"It's something I picked up from Billy."

"He's a bad influence, didn't I tell you?"

"You're late."

"You could do a lot better. Anyway, I'm right on time. You weren't there."

"Billy's none of you business." He scratched his neck.

Sonia thought, *He's going to break out in a rash if he keeps this up.*

She could hear the Indian dance song. "That's awful."

"I saw part of the first show. It looks okay. That music is a Bollywood opening."

"Hollywood. Are you drunk?"

"Bollywood, Sonia. It's an East Indian, well, an Arabic dance tune in an Indian movie. You're missing it."

"It's an Indian movie?"

"No, just the opening song."

He closed the safe door without locking it and walked over to Sonia. He fished out the pen flashlight in his pocket and took her arm.

"Come on. I'll take you to your seat."

When she turned, he pointed to the spot on her dress and asked, "What happened?"

"I sat down on the sidewalk to wait for the bus."

He shook his head and reached for a cloth from a pile on a cabinet that he used to clean the lobby doors.

She had lost her interest in the movie.

"What's wrong?" he asked.

"Tired." She was looking up at the top of the stairs. If Asim noticed, he didn't say anything.

"Maybe I'll pass on *Ghost World*," she said.

He was insistent, and she didn't have the stamina to protest. He escorted her down the aisle and shined the pen light down the row she liked and covered the seat with the towel and waited until she settled in before leaving.

On the screen were hundreds of high school graduates in caps and gowns, while on stage, a girl in a wheelchair, her head and torso tethered to traction devices, was talking platitudes—"high school is like the training wheels for the bicycle of real life." Sonia thought: *I don't like kids.* But Enid, with the black work boots and "Raptor" T-shirt interested her. She thought the diner in the next scene would be a good place to eat and remembered the movie with the boys in Baltimore who sat in a diner and wisecracked about their lives and didn't see they weren't going anywhere. But that was a different movie. She should be paying attention to *Ghost World*. She didn't know what was happening to her. By the time Enid got the idea of calling some poor love-starved stranger and left the message on his machine—"Hi, it's me, your striking blonde. Of course I remember you."—Sonia was relieved. The movie, finally, had snared her.

MARY ON THE WALL

LATER THAT NIGHT, not long before the movie ended, Billy returned. He wore a ratty T-shirt with Jim Kelly's name and the number twelve across it. His hair was standing in thick, splayed bristles, as if he had been running his fingers through it. He looked like shit.

Asim asked, "What happened?"

"A kid at the home stabbed Father Laferette."

"Why?"

"The priest used to be a Bengal Bouts boxer at Notre Dame. No one suspected—"

"Bengal Bouts?" Asim interrupted.

Billy wasn't listening, and said, "His name is Joey. He ran into my room and locked the door. He sat in a chair and said, 'I think I killed Laferette.' He wouldn't say anything else. For about five minutes he just sat on the bed. Then the cops broke in."

"Why did he run into your room?"

"You think I had something going with the kid?" Billy looked incredulous. "Jesus, I don't fool around with kids."

Asim hadn't meant to make things worse. He put his arms around Billy, and whispered, "I'm sorry. You okay?"

Billy relaxed.

"When I got back to the home after leaving here, Joey came to see me. He told me the priest had raped him. I told him that he needed to report it. I told the kid if he didn't, I would. I told him Father Baker would have wanted him to tell. I told him Our Lady would want him to. He was scared."

"Our Lady?"

"These kids believe in her. They may think everything sucks, no one gives a shit, but they believe in her. I've seen her too. She looks like Sinead O'Connor."

"You've seen her?"

"I saw her on the wall above the lampshade. She told me we would be very happy together."

"You talk to her."

"Why not."

Asim scratched at his neck like he had with Sonia, like he does whenever he's restless, and said, "You're scaring me."

"She doesn't agree with the Church about fags. All that matters, she told me, is love."

Asim looked helpless, and thought, *He's talking about love and seeing a woman on the wall. Great.*

"Before he left my room, I told the kid about Mary on the wall. He wasn't surprised. He said he talks to her all the time. He agreed she looks like Sinead O'Connor. Joey said she told him it was okay to do whatever he had to. I didn't know that meant stabbing Laferette. He said he'd tell Father Justin, but first he had to get something from his room. He asked me whether I would go with him when he got back. Of course, I told him. Ten minutes later he rushed in and locked the door and told me he thought he had killed Laferette."

"What happened to the priest?"

"He's in the hospital. He's going to be okay."

Asim didn't want to think it, but he did, *Don't I have enough to worry about?* "Wait here. I have to clear the theater. Then we can go somewhere."

Billy sat in the chair next to the Sabrina poster. He said, "Let's go to the park and look at the lake."

"Okay."

When Asim got to the lobby, Lucy was hanging around as if she was expecting him. He had forgotten about Sonia.

Asim said. "You stayed for both shows."

"I told you I like Thora Birch. My father's picking me up."

"He's coming here?"

"He said he might want to talk to you."

"I'm not talking to him. Just stay outside. I've got to lock the doors."

Tony walked by and said, "*Jeepers Creepers* is available and you get *Ghost World*. Gotta run. The old lady wants to watch the Northern Lights. We'll take a couple of lawn chairs to Lake Erie."

"That's sweet," Lucy said.

"Who are you?" Tony asked.

"Lucy," Asim said.

Tony raised an eyebrow and asked, "A girlfriend?"

"A friend," Lucy said.

"Ciao," he said. "You are more like your father every day."

Asim wondered what his father would think about Billy. He wondered whether the old man would think Lucy was pretty. *A threesome,* he thought, *I'm not interested. I'm not my father.* He pictured the kid stabbing the priest and Billy talking to Mary on the wall and Tarik's threats and the skull. He didn't know why everything had gotten out of control.

A Ford Explorer pulled up and someone powered down the passenger window and waved.

"Come on, I'll introduce you," she said.

"Get lost."

She looked surprised and got into the van.

Asim turned and went inside.

He remembered Sonia and worried that something might have happened to her. She had never stayed in her seat after a movie. *Jesus,* he thought, *Tarik has taken her.*

He checked the seat. She wasn't there. He checked the restroom—empty. And then he thought, *The office.*

When he walked in he saw that she was holding Billy's arm, and on the desk was the skull, which Billy must have removed from the open safe.

Billy asked, "What's going on? There's this skull; it's full of ashes."

"It's only a skull," Sonia said.

Masika appeared in the doorway. Before she noticed anything, she said, "All the marquee lights are still lit."

Asim told her, "Tarik's back. He left me this."

"Call the police," she said.

SOMETHING'S SWIMMING IN THE SKY

ASIM STAYED BEHIND at The Bethlehem with Billy. On the way home with Masika, Sonia said: "Tarik is like your mother, Sinai crazy."

Masika gave her a look and said, "That's what father used to say."

"I don't believe in any god anymore," Sonia said.

They were at a light on Ridge and Rosary.

"Stupid name for a street," Sonia said.

"What?"

"Maybe it was supposed to be Rotary and some Catholic crazy changed it to Rosary."

They could see the dome of Our Lady of Victory blocks away lit above the rooftops. The traffic light cast a red glare across the dash.

Masika said: "He didn't have a beard until he started going to the mosque and hanging out at Ferran's. A few years ago, he'd never even stepped foot in the mosque. He spent a lot of time watching videos in his room. He watched a lot of porn. If he were going crazy, I never would have guessed it was crazy for God."

Sonia was looking out the window at nothing in particular.

Masika started off again. "I don't know anything about Islam. I don't know how he started with it."

Sonia asked, "With what?"

"Islam."

They were talking past each other, which was the case more often now that Sonia couldn't keep her concentration on any one thing for long.

They pulled into the driveway beside a police cruiser. Light from inside pulsated so that it looked threatening.

Sgt. Pelligrino, the cop who used to take Sonia to her apartment after she'd wandered off, got out and walked to their car.

"Mrs. Markovich, I tracked you down." He was carrying a box. "I didn't know what happened to you after the fire."

"What's wrong, officer?" Masika said.

"Nothing's wrong. I've got something for Mrs. Markovich."

"This late," Masika said suspiciously.

"I should have called first, you're right."

"I like visitors," Sonia said. "Are those lights swimming in the sky?"

Masika and Sonia stuck their heads out the windows. Everyone looked up.

"I don't see anything 'swimming.' You mean the stars? Someone at the station said something about the Northern Lights. Maybe that's what you saw," the cop said.

"You want a brandy, officer?" Sonia asked. She thought, *Northern Lights.*

He laughed. "I'm working."

Sonia smiled, flirting.

"Maybe some other time," he said.

"You said you had something for Sonia," Masika said.

"That's right. The people who live in her old house called me a while ago and said they found a cranny in a closet wall that was packed with some stuff that belonged to her mother and father, I guess. They asked me if I'd give it to her."

Sonia said, "Another box. Maybe another skull."

"What?" the cop asked.

"Never mind," Masika whispered. "She doesn't always make sense." She got out of the car and walked to the other side and opened the door for Sonia.

"That's a funny name for a vehicle," Sonia said.

"What are you talking about?" Masika asked.

"The Bubble Brush van that just drove by."

Masika shook her head and said, "Let's go inside."

The cop followed and repeated, "I should have called."

"It's okay," Masika said.

"I know you," Sonia said.

"Of course you do. I used to help you find your way home. You called me Fred. I don't know why."

"Who's Fred?"

"You don't remember," he said.

All she could think of was Fred MacMurray and he didn't look at all like Richard Myles in *Above Suspicion* or Walter Neff in *Double Indemnity*.

Sonia felt bad because he sounded disappointed. She said, "Not everyone can be a matinee idol."

He laughed and gave Masika the box.

"What's that?" Sonia asked.

"The stuff your parents left behind," he said.

She frowned, as if she were aware for the first time that she was confused.

"I'm glad you've got some company. Call me if you need anything, Mrs. Markovich."

"Company," she said. "Who's got company?"

"He means me, Sonia—and Asim."

"Asim's here?" she asked.

Masika shook her head again, and went inside.

Sonia stood on the porch watching the cop return to his cruiser. She waved. He stuck his head out of the window and said, "I hope the stuff brings back some memories."

Her hand was still in the air.

"I'll call next time," he said. The cruiser was at the end of the drive, its taillights blinking.

She looked up again and said, "Lights are still swimming in the sky."

No one heard her.

She thought the sky looked like an enormous movie screen. She remembered Badru telling her: *It's almost a way of living, going to the movies every week. New ones, old ones, funny, heartbreaking, dreamy and terrifying.*

She watched a while longer and then thought, *Stupid me. It's not a movie screen at all; it's just the sky.*

Masika called from inside.

"Sonia," she shouted. "Let's see what we have here."

Sonia stood on the porch and watched the cruiser disappear down the street. She went inside.

"Let's put in a movie," she said.

"You just saw *Ghost World*. I'd like to have a look in this box."

"I wish your father could see us now."

Masika patted Sonia's arm, and then pulled out a photograph of a man with a wooden leg and thick gray beard. He was standing beside a plank. "Who's this? Your father?"

Sonia darted forward and said, "That's Yuri, my grandfather, not the bastard."

"Bastard?" Masika asked.

"I think my mother hated my father."

"What about you?"

"I hated him for a long time too." She paused. "In the end, that's how my mother referred to him—'bastard.' I guess he was."

She tried to picture her father but it felt as if her mind had blocked the memory, and then she cringed because she worried the disease was eating away at everything.

"I can't see him anymore."

Masika didn't know what to say.

"Nicky's worse than my father. It's worse when a man hurts you and you still can't stop seeing him. Badru understood."

"My father wasn't a saint."

"Don't be so grumpy."

Masika reached back into the box.

"Here's a record, *Bye-Bye-Blackbird*."

Sonia took the 45, still in the jacket—deep red with a blackbird in flight. She thought of the sad sack with all of the records in *Ghost World*.

"I remember this," she said.

The phone rang and Masika left to answer it. It was the doctor. "I'm going upstairs to take this, Sonia."

She started humming *Blackbird* and picked through more of the stuff in the box. She fished out a poem that her mother had written. She thought she remembered it but wasn't sure:

I arrived in Lackawanna
and watched the flames
shoot from smokestacks
of Bethlehem Steel.
Back in Russia,
Wolves fled the forest.
The dead coughed.
Dogs ate dogs.
The holy mother said,
"Waters near Greece are clean."

The czar hanged my great-grandfather.
The rope split and he lived.
Still winter dreams darken beds.
Children are cold.

Our Lady promised dances in the field.
Fire and ash fly everywhere.

My dreams are bad.
I hug death and rub my loins.
Boys in their cradles cuddle worms.

On a cliff wolves gathered around a naked child.
No human sound anywhere, just wind
and the rustle of wolves' feet.
Children are wild in the mountains,
hunt rabbits and are hunted by bears.

A prince killed his daughter
for a harvest feast.
He gave her sweet wine,
poppies and rose petals,
linen for innocence.
Men dismembered her,
undid her flesh,
scattered her bones
in the fallow field.

In the morning the back door
opens to a woman
standing in fog. She looks
like my dead mother.
She's holding a spade,
and says, "We must bury
the bad men. We must kill them now."

We must bury the bad men.
Who are the men with yellow eyes?
Why are bedrooms filled with bones?
Do you hear the bells on the troika?
The perezvon, dying echo.
Sounds of bad men coming.

Sonia closed her eyes and imagined a dead woman naked in the snow. Something like a half-dog, half-bear was tearing off the corpse's arms and legs with red devil's paws. A blackbird circled. Her mother had told her stories of old Russia all of the time. Sometimes they made her shiver. She was tired, and she wanted sleep.

She walked upstairs and removed her dowdy dress, surprised she didn't have to struggle. Without bending, she kicked off her shoes. She could hear Masika on the phone. She thought, *I can't help it if Badru wasn't happy with the Egyptian.* In her bra and silk panties, she lay in bed. She touched her sex and whispered *Nicky.* Paused and whispered, *Badru.* She pictured Asim somewhere with Billy, and thought, *Let them have their fun. The redhead isn't so bad.*

ANGELS WITH TRUMPETS

ASIM COULDN'T BELIEVE a day could end with so much trouble. While he locked the lobby doors, he noticed Billy was watching from the Pig Iron. He crossed the street and could smell cigarette smoke from the bar's open window. Billy, his arms crossed like a bodyguard, nodded to Asim.

The jukebox was playing Elvis Presley: *Love me tender, love me dear, tell me you are mine, I'll be yours through all the years, til the end of time.*

"I've been looking out for that black Arab," Billy said.

"Muslim," Asim said.

"What?"

"He wasn't Arab, he was a black American, probably a guy just out of prison, a jailhouse conversion. I bet Tarik gave him the cap and paid him to deliver the note. He's just a messenger."

"What did Tarik say?"

"He wants me to meet him in Niagara Falls. He didn't say why."

"You're not going."

Asim didn't want to argue and said, "I thought we were going to the park."

"I needed a beer first."

"You used to drink a lot more."

"That was before I met you."

Asim smiled. "It's been a rotten day for both of us. This place stinks. I can't take the smoke. Let's go."

Billy nodded, in the way Asim knew he was being indulged. "You're the boss," Billy said.

They walked the mile or so to South Park, and for the first time, where drivers could see, Asim wanted to take Billy's hand. But he didn't.

Billy asked, "Why do you think Tarik sent him? Why would your brother give you that thing?"

Asim remembered the imam's video of the Cole and fighters in the desert shooting at posters of Bill Clinton. Billy didn't know about it.

"You saw the skull and heard him on the tape. Whatever he wants from me, it's trouble."

A car honked and someone shouted, "Hey, sweeties."

They looked up, and Billy flipped the guy a finger.

"That's the way to start something," Asim said.

"Who the fuck cares? I'm tired of that shit. And I'm serious. You're not meeting Tarik, at least not alone."

Asim wondered whether he should have told Billy anything and worried his hotheadedness would make things worse.

Billy said, "When I'm finished with your brother, he'll get the next plane back to Egypt."

"Afghanistan."

"What's the difference?"

"He's not going anywhere as long as he thinks I screwed him."

"How?"

"The video."

"What video?"

"Months ago, the day Tarik left, he came to the theater with an imam who asked me to deliver a video and a lot of money to a mosque in Toronto. I didn't do it."

"That got Tarik into trouble?"

"That's what he says. Now he wants me to pay for screwing him, and other things."

"What other things?"

"Are you clueless? You heard him. He hates gays, he hates Sonia, and he wants me to pay for crimes against Allah. He's crazy."

"Where's the video?" Billy's concern was intensifying.

"It's at the theater."

"I want to see it. Let's go back."

"Tomorrow. I've had enough tonight."

They were getting close to the park and Billy, calmer, said, "I won't let anything happen to you."

Asim thought, *Okay*, and for a moment he believed that might be true.

"So what do you think about Michigan?" Asim asked.

"Michigan. Why?"

"I don't know. Changing the subject, I guess."

"Christ, I want to help you. Don't you get it?" Billy said.

"Can't we just go to the park and forget everything for a while?" Billy rolled his eyes.

Across the street was Our Lady of Victory Basilica, a miniature St. Peter's. On each side were half-moon porticos with columns shining in yellow light; a statue of Our Lady of Victory, ten feet high, stood above the main doors while, recessed behind her, the basilica's dome ballooned into the night—angels with trumpets circled it.

"No one's out," Asim said.

"They're in the woods."

Asim wasn't listening. "I love it in the park." He raised his arm and pointed. "I like to sit there, right on the edge of the evergreens. From that bench, all you can see is the dome lit like a spaceship behind you and the lake out there."

"Like *The Day the Earth Stood Still*," Billy said.

"Aren't *you* the movie buff?"

"Shithead."

"What are you going to do about the kid?" Asim asked.

"Why should I do anything?"

"Because you were the one he ran to."

"There's nothing anyone can do," Billy said.

"Maybe you can talk to his family."

"He's a Father Baker orphan. He doesn't have a family."

A man walked by and stopped near a break in the trees and looked back. He nodded and walked into the woods.

"You used to nod," Asim said.

Billy arched his eyebrows.

"I used to sit here and watch you nod at guys who walked by. Once you nodded at me. You didn't notice, but I nodded back," Asim said.

"I saw. I thought you were jailbait. You made me shy."

" Right, *you* shy. You don't really talk to Mary on the wall?"

He smiled. "You bet I do."

Asim considered asking Billy to take him into the woods. He liked the smell of the evergreen needles on the ground and their cushiony feel underfoot and the moist lake air that swept in. He had never been fucked before Billy. He had never kissed a guy. Sometimes he would sit on the bench or walk close to the brush and needles and listen for voices inside: men whispering, moaning. A few shouted. Once he heard a guy weeping.

"Do you want to go inside?" Asim asked.

"With you, in there?"

"I guess."

"Why?"

"Why do you think?"

"That's for closet queens, *honey*." Billy arched his brows again, and smiled. Asim liked it when Billy dropped his masculinity and feigned a theatrical air.

At that moment, Asim knew he wanted sex more than anything.

He heard footsteps and looked up. In the lot, he saw an Explorer, and then he saw Lucy's father at the edge of the park.

"Fuck," Asim said.

"You want to fuck inside there. Aren't you the dirty little whore all of a sudden," Billy said.

"That guy. He's Lucy's dad."

"Who's Lucy?"

"A girl from school. She was at the movie tonight. Her father's an FBI agent."

"An FBI agent, Jesus."

He could tell Billy wasn't processing everything.

The FBI guy walked up and said, "Hi, boys. It's late to be in the park." Turning to Asim, he said, "I'm Lucy's dad, Gerry Akorn. She told you I wanted to talk to you."

"I recognized the Explorer," Asim said.

"Observant. That's good."

"Who do you think you are?" Billy asked. "It's after midnight. You don't have any right to shadow us."

Asim shook his head and said, "He's quick-tempered. Protective, too."

Akorn stared Billy down and said, "I'm a friend, so don't get belligerent without knowing what's going on. Asim needs a friend like me. Who are you?"

"This is Billy. He's *really* a friend."

"So I guess you need all the friends you can get. Lucy thinks you're great."

Asim didn't say anything.

Billy fidgeted with a coat button.

"Have you seen your brother?"

"No."

Billy gave Asim a look, but didn't say anything. Then he coughed for attention but Asim ignored him.

"So, any contact with him?" Akorn asked.

"No."

Billy said Asim's name.

"Stay out of this, Billy," Asim said.

Billy scowled.

"So you know where he went?" Akorn asked.

"He's in Pakistan. He took off with Ferran from the mosque and an imam named Shamal in February. That's all I know."

"So you know Shamal?"

"Tarik brought him to the theater. They took some money. I didn't like him. I don't like imams, period," Asim said.

"*So* wait a minute, *mister so,*" Billy said. "Why are you grilling him about his brother?"

"It's okay, Billy. Don't make any trouble."

Akorn looked at Asim and said, "Let's walk over there by the fountain and talk. You don't have to be afraid of me."

"You're not taking him anywhere," Billy said.

"He can hear whatever you want to tell me," Asim said.

"We think your brother's back."

"If he's back, he didn't come home," Asim said.

"So he didn't try to reach you?"

"No."

Asim glanced at Billy, who looked like he was going to spoil everything.

"What about Masika and the old lady?"

"Jesus, this guy thinks he knows a lot," Billy said. "Fuckin' FBI doesn't have anything better to do than butt into a family fight."

"Shut up, Billy," Asim said.

Akorn paused and said, irritated, "So you think I'm stupid. The old lady whose apartment burned down in February—why is she staying with you? Wasn't that when your brother left town? Has he tried to reach your sister or the old lady? Why are you so close to her?"

"Maybe he should get a lawyer before he talks to you anymore," Billy said. This time they both ignored him.

"My father used to take care of Sonia, kinda. After the fire, we took her in. She doesn't know anything about Tarik. Even my sister and I don't know much. He's a loner."

"Did he ever talk to you about Afghanistan?" Akorn asked.

"Never."

"Nothing about training in the desert? Militants?"

Billy looked helpless.

"What kind of militants?" Asim asked.

"The kind who blow things up." He reached into a pocket and pulled something out. "Cops found this in an airport in Toronto. Do you recognize it?"

He handed Asim a still of Travis Bickle. Billy leaned in to see.

"Robert DeNiro. From *Taxi Driver*," Asim said.

"Read the back," Akorn said.

"I'm God's lonely man. Faggots and the Russian bitch will hear from me."

Billy took it, and said, "What's going on?"

Asim tried hard to keep his hands from shaking. His head hurt.

Akorn took back the photo, turned to Asim, and said, "So you've seen this before."

"No. I just know it's DeNiro."

"It was inside a bag with stuff that belonged to your brother."

"That's his handwriting, I can tell," Asim said.

"What does he mean?"

"I guess he hates gays and Russians."

"You guess."

"No. I know he hates gays—I mean—I don't know what he has against Sonia."

"Yes you do. You're just not telling me."

Asim didn't say anything.

"Why would he go all the way to Afghanistan because he hates homosexuals?" Billy asked.

"Islam," Asim said. "He said something about how the Koran thinks gays deserve to die. He talked about doctors in Egypt who cut off a gay man's balls. Religion made him crazy."

"But what about the old lady? What's with her?" Akorn asked.

"I don't know. It must be *personal*. I told you, he didn't talk much." Asim thought, *What am I going to say? Tarik hates Sonia because she loved our father and let her husband and our father fuck each other. He hates me because I'm a fag.*

Asim was sweating under his shirt. He knew he had said too much.

Someone walked out of the evergreen patch and another guy followed. Akorn looked at Billy and Asim and didn't say anything.

"So, you guys go home." He touched Asim's shoulder and said, "Sometime next week I'm going to ask you to come down to the office in Buffalo for a talk. Bring your sister and the old lady. As long as Tarik is missing, you're in trouble, too. You're better off talking to me than to someone else."

He fished into his pocket, took out his wallet, and handed Asim a card.

"Call me if you hear something sooner. And do me a favor. Go straight home."

He returned to the Explorer and they watched him drive off. Asim thought, *I wonder what he's going to tell Lucy.*

"Why didn't you tell him about the skull and the tape and Tarik's note? Jesus, what's this about cutting off an Egyptian's balls?" Billy asked.

"I thought you got it. Tarik will kill Sonia if he finds out I've been talking to the cops. He probably wants to kill us, too." Asim was trembling.

"It's okay," Billy said. He leaned in and kissed Asim's forehead.

Asim said, "I don't want to go home."

"We'll go back to Father Baker's. You can stay the night. I don't want to be alone either."

Another couple slipped out of the evergreens. They looked at Asim and then turned and walked off.

"Everyone's so lonely," Asim said.

"What do you mean?"

"We knew Tarik was screwed up. We didn't do anything."

"Sometimes you can't do anything. I should know."

He knew Billy was thinking about his parents, maybe the kid.

"Let's go," Billy said. "It's only the lonely, you and me, buddy."

They walked past Our Lady of Victory and turned down Baker Alley to the Protectory.

"That's a weird name for the building, considering Father Laferette," Asim said.

Billy nodded. "Wait here a second."

He opened the door and walked inside while Asim leaned against a statue of a friar in a robe and sandals.

Billy came back. "It's okay. Everyone's asleep."

The hallway floor was marble and lined with paintings and sculptures. Billy pointed to a stone angel tucked under the staircase.

"Cute, isn't he?" he whispered.

"There's no Mary anywhere."

"Mary's an apparition," Billy whispered. "She comes and goes."

Asim didn't know what to say.

The room was at the end of the hall on the second floor. Before going inside Billy whispered, "If you have to piss or something, you better go now. That's the bathroom door. I'll stand out here and make sure no one goes in."

Inside was a line of three urinals and a couple of stalls, like in a school. While he was pissing, someone, wearing pajamas, came out of a stall and walked on without a glance at Asim.

"He saw me," Asim said, when he walked out.

"That's Father William. He sleepwalks and doesn't remember anything of where he's been. Even taking a shit apparently doesn't wake him."

Billy opened his door. The lock was missing.

"You can't lock it. What if someone catches us?"

"The priests wouldn't walk in unannounced. What they don't see, they don't find. It's a good way to deal with church contradictions."

As soon as he closed the door, Billy kissed Asim. Their eyes had not adjusted to the dark. He pressed Asim against the door, and whispered, "I never loved anyone before." Even the words felt sexy.

Asim thought, *What am I going to do?*

"You heard me, right?" Billy said.

"I want to go to Michigan," Asim said.

"Again with Michigan," Billy said, kissing his ear.

"Would you go with me?" He said it low enough that he knew Billy probably had not heard him. If Billy had, he didn't say anything.

Asim touched Billy's cock and pictured his brother standing nearby, holding a scalpel.

"Tarik's never going to leave me alone," he said. "That's one of the reasons I want to go to Michigan. And I want to study film. Maybe make a movie."

"You should be *in* a movie," Billy said, pulling off Asim's shirt. "Forget about your brother. He can't hurt you if I'm around."

Billy backed away and unbuckled his jeans, pulled them down, and stepped out. He slipped off his briefs and stepped up and pulled down Asim's khakis, with boxers bunched inside. He knelt and took Asim in his mouth.

Asim imagined free-falling in a night sky.

Billy nudged Asim onto the bed and raised himself, inching lower until their flesh slithered in the muggy air. He entered Asim and started singing Elvis softly: *Love me tender, love me dear, tell me you are mine, I'll be yours through all the years, til the end of time.*

Asim wasn't listening. All he wanted was Billy deep inside him.

NATIONAL GEOGRAPHIC

SONIA WOKE IN THE middle of the night with a vision of Randolph Scott in her head. She had dreamed about *Ride Lonesome* and remembered that she and Nicky made love after seeing the movie. Scott stood by the burning tree where years before Lee Van Cleef had murdered Scott's wife. The movie was filled with gunslingers, killers, pretty Karen Steele, the revenge-bent Scott—all on a stagecoach depending on one another to keep themselves safe from Indians while they knew they couldn't really trust one another because each one wanted something different, and everyone was basically alone. After the movie Nicky, in one of his sweet and tender moods, told her he loved the word "lonesome," the way the letter "m" wants sweetness that the nagging "n" won't let it have. He said the "m" wants to roll off somewhere like tumbleweed, anywhere, except the "n" is always tugging, saying "no" and "nothing" to what the "m" desires.

She lay in bed and touched herself. This time she imagined she was alone with Badru. She saw him in the mirror. He stood before her and unbuttoned his shirt and pulled it off; he slipped off his pants and let them fall to the floor. She didn't care if this was the Sinai crazy's room. She should have been Badru's wife anyway. She would have divorced Nicky. Asim would have been her son. If Badru wanted to fuck Nicky, even after they were married, she would have let him. She understood love was hard to find, and if it had to be shared, she was willing.

Sonia looked around the bedroom. She had arranged her own things: bus tokens, movie stubs, dried dandelions and lavender stems, perfumes, lipsticks, powder, bracelets, hair pins, rings, pill bottles. In the corner of the mirror was a photograph of Nicky and Badru. She had found it on the floor in the closet, wiped off a sticky, dusty film as best she could, and slid it into the edge of the mirror. She was glad that Nicky did not step out of the photograph. *He's always known when to leave us alone,* she thought. She kissed Badru, ran the back of her hand down his olive chest, guided his fingers between her legs. Dark and exotic, he didn't resemble Randolph Scott or Lee Van Cleef, and she was almost happy until she looked into the glass and saw she was alone, the photograph curling, her hand inside her panties.

She rose and went downstairs. She turned on a light. On the
shelf in the living room were rows of *National Geographic*s. She
picked one out—November 1978—and sat on the couch. The light
was dim and she struggled to see as she flipped pages: a moose in
Maine; naked Nigerian women; a Tasmanian field of eucalyptus,
which she had never seen before. The trees were gigantic, four hundred feet high, with leathery, lance-shaped leaves, puffball flowers
red and orange with bees swirling everywhere, and bark dappled
gray, green, russet, cream peeling like the skin of an enormous
standing python. There were Australian tiger and angel fish, bar-
racuda. At the back of the magazine was a story about Crow
Agency, Montana, where rooftops were lined with the stiff-backed
birds, and she imagined everywhere the sound of pecking like
hammering. The tumbleweed was skeletal. Crows unfolded their
wings above a boy walking to his one-room schoolhouse and at
noon followed a farmer down the street on his way to the diner.
About a dozen crows perched on the edge of a trough for horses
and stayed there until the sun set, their attention on an old couple
who had fallen asleep on the porch while a *Bonanza* rerun flickered
on a television. She put down the magazine and said, "I don't know
what my mother saw in black birds. You can have them."

She was tired and stretched herself out on the couch. She noticed her feet twitching, her hands shaking. She didn't know what
to do next. She thought about checking to see if Asim had returned
but decided not to. *He'll never be my son*, she thought. *How can a boy
I dream about naked be my son?* She didn't remember Masika upstairs. She forgot about the cop and the box. The photographs, her
mother's poem, the skull, Jehovah Witnesses on the bus—every-

thing from the day had vanished. She didn't know where she was. But she could see, if "see" was the right way to describe what she sensed, Nicky and Badru. They were beautiful. They were hugging each other, calling her. She closed her eyes and slept.

Sunday, September 9, 2001
MAID OF THE MIST

ASIM STOOD ON THE walk outside the theater and studied the parked cars. No beat-up Volvo, no Ford Explorer with tinted windows, no white van. If someone was watching, he couldn't tell. He went inside the lobby and locked the door. The poster, *From Hell*, showed Johnny Depp peering alongside a zigzag slash of red that looked like the tear that a saw might make.

The night before, Sonia had walked out of the movie, saying, "I don't have the stomach for it."

He didn't like it either. The prostitutes didn't look as he had imagined London whores in the Ripper's time. They were clean country girls, and no one, except the brooding Depp, seemed as if they belonged in the fog-shrouded London slum. Asim didn't have the stomach for the murders—rasps, scalpels, forceps, drill bits gleaming in a red-satin case; a liver, pancreas, kidney, or heart in the Ripper's hand. He thought of Tarik when the Ripper, accused in a secret court, said: "Someday man will look back and understand I gave birth to the new century."

After she had left the movie, Sonia said she wanted to wait upstairs and rest on the cot. Asim was uncharacteristically impatient (he had been going over in his head the meeting he would have with Tarik), and he almost shot out, *your lover boy is dead!* But the way she grabbed the railing worried him. When he tried to help, she insisted she could make it, clutching the rail and ascending one impossible step at a time. Asim shouted to her that the room was open, but if she heard, she didn't acknowledge it, and shuffled off. Later, after he had closed the theater, he found her lying on the cot, her blouse open. She was staring at the ceiling, and for a few frantic moments, he thought she wasn't breathing. He tapped her shoulder, and she darted forward, barely recognizing him. Her wrinkled breasts unnerved him. He helped her up, buttoned her blouse, and hugged her; she was cold, unresponsive. He thought, *Why did my father have to die? He should be taking care of her.*

He got her into the car, and on the way home she remained speechless. He called Masika from her room to help, and by the time she came out Sonia was talking. Masika said she would take Sonia to Deaconess in the morning but Asim wondered whether she should have been checked that night. Sonia protested, and shaking wildly, she shouted, "Can't you see I'm fine. Leave me alone." Asim had never heard her shout before. Masika told her not to worry and held her close while helping her up the stairs.

When they woke, Sonia was already in the kitchen eating a

poached egg. She greeted them and said, "Did Asim tell you? The movie wasn't any good."

He had thought, *I can't worry about her now. There's too much to do.*

Masika said, "I don't think we should take her to see the FBI agent this week. She barely knows Tarik."

"What FBI?" Sonia asked.

"Never mind," Masika said.

"He's a bastard. I'll tell the FBI he's a bastard."

Masika shook her head, and said, "Eat your egg, Sonia."

"We'll go alone," Asim whispered to his sister.

He had not told his sister anything about Tarik's note and the summons to Niagara Falls. He knew she would have called the cops if she had known.

Inside the theater office, he remembered that he had left his knapsack in the car. When he returned for it, he looked down Abbott Road and didn't see anyone, not his brother, not Lucy's father, not a Muslim stranger who looked like he could blow something to bits. It was a little past noon. The Pig Iron had reopened. He saw a few men, old guys with scruffy beards, drinking first shots of the day. *Billy could grow old like them, especially without me,* he thought, *What am I going to do about Billy?* He reached into the Cadillac and grabbed his knapsack and let it dangle, empty, along his shoulder. He paused before crossing and looked at the marquee:

BETHLEHEM THEATER

FROM HELL 7:00 AND 9:00

Isn't that the truth, he thought.

It was too late to go to Michigan this fall, but he could start in January. He would sell the theater to an Iranian who wanted to turn it into a rug showroom. Masika had agreed. He didn't know whether Billy would want to come or even whether he wanted Billy to. And there was Sonia. She wouldn't be up for many more openers at the Bethlehem even if he kept it going. He thought, *She shakes so much, her mind's so scattered, movies won't save her from everything she's lost.* He believed his father would have understood, and thought: *I'll make a movie about the Bethlehem. A* Cinema Paradiso *thing. Except my movie will be a romantic comedy and everyone will leave happy the way* Singin' in the Rain *leaves everyone wanting to dance. At the beginning of the credits, this will be the dedication: To Sonia, Nicky, and my father.*

He felt a tap on his shoulder. He reared back and accidentally elbowed a woman, pale and plainly dressed.

"Who are you?" he asked.

"Excuse me," she said. She handed him a pamphlet titled "Is There a Creator Who Cares about You?"

He gave her a look.

"I saw you gazing at the marquee. You seem troubled. That movie is an *abomination,* isn't it?"

Does every religious nut use that word? he thought. He checked the pamphlet, shook his head, and said, "Your creator is a joke." He left.

Inside the lobby, he watched her and thought she looked like she was praying.

Back in the office, he eyed the photograph of Humphrey Bogart in Rick's Café Américain. He imagined his father sitting at a smoky table, woozy from too much booze, saying, "You'll never get out of Lackawanna. You'll die in Lackawanna." He imagined being Rick Blaine and Billy coming up to his table and the conversation:

Where were you last night?

That's so long ago. I don't remember.

Will I see you tonight?

I never make plans that far ahead.

He was sad to play it so cool because Billy would walk away, with no one to love and that would be his fault.

He looked at his watch. It was getting late and he had to leave. He would meet Tarik and show his brother he wasn't afraid. That would be a start.

He leaned forward, turned the safe dial left and heard the click of the cylinder as if it were a gun chamber engaging, turned the dial slowly right, left again, right until the lock released. He was so uneasy that everything was heightened in his mind, happening in slow motion. He heard the sound of the iron door opening more loudly than it actually did. His hand felt heavy. He fished out the Cole tape and the note from the imam. He grabbed the carved-out rim of the skull and felt ashes on his fingertips and lifted the thing, cupping the bottom in his free hand before placing it on the desk. He cringed. He removed the plastic bag from the trash can and dropped in the video, then the skull, which turned over, spilling ashes into the bag. He wiped his fingertips with the inside of the plastic and placed everything in the knapsack. He repositioned it, heavier now, on his shoulder. When he passed the *From Hell* poster, he imagined Johnny Depp nodding.

Back on the street he forgot to look for the van or Explorer or anyone suspicious. An old Polish guy named Stan waved from the Pig Iron window. The guy had often slept on a pew inside the basilica and sometimes Asim let him wash up in the Bethlehem's bathroom. He gave the guy out-of-date bridge mix and popcorn smothered in butter. When Stan didn't smell, Asim let him watch a movie. In the bar window, Stan was grinning, toothless, clenching a beer mug close to his chest. Asim nodded before driving off. He turned down Ridge and passed Our Lady of Victory and South Park where he had kissed Billy on the bench before Lucy's father showed up. He passed the DB Mart and Yemen Soccer Field and Sonia's boarded-up apartment. By then all he was thinking about was Tarik. While his brother watched, he would take the skull from the knapsack and throw it overboard. *So much for inspiration,* he would say. Tarik would get the message: he didn't want anything to do with *jihad.* Then in a couple of days he would meet with Lucy's father. He didn't care what happened to Tarik. Eventually, he would leave Lackawanna, for good.

He turned onto the Skyway near the abandoned steel mill and followed the winding elevated road along the lakeshore and across the wind-battered bridge into Buffalo, the dilapidated grain elevators and railroad yards scarring the waterfront. In the distance was the downtown: Niagara Mohawk Tower, Pilot Field, Cyclorama, the Gas Works, Temple of Music. Queen City was a stupid name for a place filled with Italian and Polish and Irish immigrants who didn't know a fuck about royalty and bashed Arabs and blacks and gays because they needed someone to hate. He caught the Robert Moses Parkway. He passed signs for West Seneca and Cheektowaga, North Tonawanda, and finally, the Niagara Reservation State Park. He wondered why so many places in Western New York, filled with white people, were named after Indians. Was it guilt? Or trophy pride? He passed billboards for Three Sisters Islands, Cave of the Winds, Goat Island, Table Rock, Devil's Hole Rapids. Finally, he saw Prospect Point and the Observation Tower where, below the cliff, the *Maid of the Mist* was waiting. He pulled off at Prospect Street, followed it to the parking lot. Ahead was the top of the concrete and steel tower where an elevator descended to the Niagara basin.

Once he was out of the car, he could hear the American and Horseshoe falls, not as deafening as the walls of water would become from the boat, but still loud enough—disharmony heard from afar, a gargantuan thrashing. Already he was coated with mist, and before slinging on the knapsack, he reached into the car for his sweatshirt. He hoisted the knapsack over his shoulder and fitted his arms into it. He thought he felt the skull dig into his scapula. He stopped, readjusted, and listened. The roar was inescapable. The sun was trying to shine through the mist and he could see patches of blue when the wind cleared the air momentarily. He saw a rainbow fade in the gauzy sky. He searched the parking lot: still no rusted Volvo, no white van, no Explorer. *Maybe Tarik won't show,* he thought.

As he got closer to the tower, the Niagara grew more resounding. A bunch of children swarmed, gigantic Twist o' the Mist ice-cream cones in their hands. There were hundreds of tourists at the tower, most of them leaving, and Asim thought of *North by Northwest,* Cary Grant urging James Mason to give up Eva Marie Saint in the cafeteria at Mount Rushmore. He looked around again to see if he could recognize anyone, maybe Lucy's father. Maybe the FBI was tailing him. For a moment a priest with a cap and hood had caught his eyes but turned away quickly. Asim wondered whether his brother wouldn't show himself until he was on the boat, probably just before the *Maid of the Mist* returned and docked so that if Tarik thought he was cornered, he would have a chance to escape. But where would his brother run to? The only way out was up the tower elevator. Asim thought, *If he's coming at all, he's coming fearless.*

He walked over to the edge of the point and saw the twin falls in the distance. He imagined Tarik standing at the lip and leaping, and thought, *It would be easier if he were dead.* An old man came up to him and asked, "Do you know why it's green?"

Asim decided he didn't have time for this guy, and didn't say anything.

"It's the massive volume of water that gives it the green color. Some people think it's vegetation. They're wrong. That's pure water."

"You know a lot about the Falls."

"I live on Rainbow Drive, less than a mile away. I grew up here. They call me Ambassador Niagara. You look foreign."

"I was born in Lackawanna."

"Too bad."

Asim smiled.

"The water below is as deep as the cliff—one hundred seventy feet."

"Really."

"Water flows over here from every one of the Great Lakes, except Superior."

Asim nodded.

"Twelve thousand years ago, she was seven miles down river."

He didn't say anything, and wondered whether his brother was watching and getting nervous because he still had not bought a ticket.

"Marilyn Monroe kissed me," the guy said.

"No shit."

"Yep. I was twenty, an extra in *Niagara*. She was running right there and fell out of a shoe. I was nearby and picked it up and gave it to her. She was supposed to be playing a conniving murderess, but, you know, she put her hand on my shoulder, so gentle, balancing herself, while she got back into her shoe. Then she kissed me. I think she said something like 'thanks' or maybe 'you're cute.' Probably just 'thanks.' I like to think she said more. She had a sweet voice. But I do know that Marilyn Monroe kissed me."

Asim decided he had better get his ticket if he was going to make the boat.

"Great story. I have to go."

"I met Arthur Miller too, about twenty years ago."

Asim waved.

He bought his ticket and thought Tarik must be waiting on the boat. He made the last elevator trip for the four-thirty sail. Sheathed in a blue plastic poncho the ticket agent had given him, he descended the gorge. Below on the rocky shore were seagulls, hundreds, cawing, and he wondered why they had chosen this deafening basin to nest in, some nursing undeterred by the hordes of tourists. He thought, *I hate birds. It can't just be Hitchcock*. The gulls' gray white coats melded into the mist. He boarded the boat on a gangplank and was surprised that there were only about a hundred people there. Before the boat left he walked around both decks and didn't see his brother or anyone who looked Arab. The stuttering black guy wasn't there. The thick mist felt like he had been inside a cloud forest for days, but the water on his skin was cold and biting. The plastic poncho didn't help. The boat pulled off the pilings and for a moment all he could smell was diesel. Soon the engines' roar was subsumed by the deafening Falls. He looked around. *A wild goose chase*, he thought. *Why the fuck did he summon me?* Then across the boat he saw Billy, who was reaching for his cap as it blew off into the rapids.

Billy was wearing black, and a priest's collar, and he was struggling to save his poncho, which he had only managed to put one arm into, from flying into the faces of an old couple. He didn't know Asim had spotted him.

Asim walked over, and astonished, asked, "What are you doing here dressed like a priest?"

The couple gave them a look and walked away.

Billy finally slipped his other arm into the poncho and said, "Don't talk to me like that. I'm worried about you. Why do you think I'm here? I don't want any asshole Arabians to hurt you."

"Arabs," Asim said. "You *know* they're Arabs."

"Who gives a shit? They're threatening you."

"I told you Tarik's behind this. No one else."

"I don't believe it."

The thrashing of the falls, even more thunderous as the boat approached, made Asim angrier. He had wanted to show Tarik he wasn't scared, and now that his brother had stood him up, he wanted to be alone. He wanted to think what he should do next.

Billy took his hand but he pulled it away.

I can't handle this, he thought. *I'm not like my father. I'm no pro-tector. I just want to be left alone.*

"You probably spoiled it," Asim said. "Tarik probably saw you following me and decided to take off. Why can't you see? I don't need your help."

Billy ignored him and asked, "How do I look?"

"Stupid."

"Admit it, you saw me and you didn't recognize me."

"Maybe you should join up. Mary on the wall is calling."

Billy didn't hear because of the noise from the falls. Spray slashed their faces. As the boat reached as close to the falls as it was going nothing was visible except cascading water, broken rocks battered by the rapids, and the insistent mist. Billy pressed the knapsack and asked, loud enough so that Asim understood, "Is it inside?"

Asim nodded and searched for the last time to see if he had missed his brother or anyone else Tarik might have sent. Then he turned and walked to the side of the boat where no passengers had gathered. The basin there was shrouded in mist too, but the falls, instead of booming inside his chest, felt like something he could manage. Billy followed him and Asim let him take his arm.

"What's the point now that Tarik didn't show? Maybe I shouldn't throw it overboard," Asim said.

"What else can you do with it?"

"It's somebody's skull."

"Whose? You don't know."

"Maybe we should give it to someone, or drop it off at the door of some funeral home, or bury it ourselves."

"Get rid of it, like you planned. You don't want the FBI knowing you've been holding on to it. It's trouble. It's creepy. It can only bring more bad things if you don't get rid of it now."

Asim nodded. "I guess."

"Don't let the ashes blow back in," Billy said.

As carefully as he could, with the wind and water lashing his back, he slipped the knapsack from his shoulders and crouched, low enough to be out of the harshest wind. He fished out the plastic bag and clamped the end with one hand. Everyone on the boat was turned toward the cascading water and didn't see him lean over the rail. He let it dangle along the side and some ashes flew out. He thought he felt some on his lips, but in this wind and mist everything tasted like the Niagara. He let it drop.

"What about the video and Tarik's tape?" Billy asked.

Asim fished them out of the knapsack. He made sure no one was looking and tossed everything.

"That's done," Billy said.

Asim wasn't listening.

Billy picked up the empty knapsack and repeated, "It's over."

Asim pictured the skull popping up somewhere along the shore of the Niagara. Maybe a kid walking along the bank with his father might find it. He said, "You're crazy if you think so."

They looked back and saw the boat arcing left on its return. A guide walked by, pointed, and shouted over the roar: "That's where the *Maid of the Mist* picked up seven-year-old Jimmy Honneycut, who fell off his uncle's motorboat on the Upper Niagara and was carried by the rapids over the Falls with just a life jacket and swimming trunks to protect him. A miracle."

Billy and Asim looked into the mist where a patch of sun was shining and a rainbow emerging.

"Isn't it romantic?" Billy asked.

Asim said, "You must be kidding."

The *Maid of the Mist* was two minutes from the dock, and Asim thought, *What if it's like the* Cole *and he's left a bomb. He knows if we jump we'll be swept into the whirlpool.*

Asim didn't warn Billy because he didn't really believe his brother would blow up the boat; still, he listened for the blast, and all he heard was the Niagara receding.

CLICKETY-CLICK

I T WAS TWO IN THE afternoon and Sonia was in bed. She didn't feel at all like Jean Harlow under the covers with a box of chocolates. Badru once told her that he had heard that Nelson Eddy sang "Ah, Sweet Mystery of Life" at the blond bombshell's funeral. Now she is lying in the earth beside Rudolph Valentino. *Nicky's not lying anywhere,* she thought. *What kind of lover am I anyway? I didn't even go to Badru's funeral. I won't look at his ashes in the urn. I'm tired of being left alone by these dead men.* When she had told Asim about this, he'd said, "What urn? He's buried at Swan Hill. You know that." She didn't know why the boy was lying. *Fathers and sons,* she thought, *they get confused about so many things. They shoot horses, don't they?*

The sheet that covered her shaking hand looked possessed. She asked her brain to stop the trembling. Her brain didn't give a shit. She hadn't been talking much the past few days and she knew her silence worried Asim and Masika. She could have talked about what didn't matter to her, as if nothing was happening, but she was tired. Her mind raced all of the time. If she stopped, she didn't know if she would miss something important. She was certain of this: things were changing fast. So she didn't say anything. She didn't know whether it was Saturday or Sunday, and she was going to break her silence and ask Asim. Then she decided it didn't matter. She thought of King Kong perched on the Empire State Building, while around the poor ape fighter planes shot him full of holes and across the screen rolled the words: "Oh, no, it wasn't the airplanes. It was beauty killed the beast." She wished she could make more sense of everything. Her mind, she knew, wasn't right. Nothing real mattered much anymore. Even Nicky and Badru had begun to recede from her memories. She would die if they disappeared forever. She would kill herself. It was the first time she'd thought of that. *Maybe it is a good idea,* she thought. She wondered where the music was coming from: the clickety, clickety, click of Gene Kelly's soft shoe: *I'm singin' in the rain, just singin' in the rain. What a glorious feeling, I'm happy again.* But she wasn't happy.

The music was coming from the Walkman that Asim had given her. He had burned a CD of her favorite songs. The phrase "favorite songs" made her think of *The Sound of Music* and Julie Andrews and then she realized she was wrong, *that* was "favorite things," not songs. She fished out the Walkman's earplug. *I'm not in the mood for love,* she thought. Then she knew she had meant to think *music. I'm not in the mood for music.* Everything was mixed up. Why didn't Asim stop by? Whose skull was that anyway? She fell asleep, listening to a buzz, from the earpiece, which she had dropped on her chest.

DON'T EAT, DON'T SLEEP, DON'T SHIT

NEXT DOOR TO THE Bubble Brush Car Wash on East Ferry in Buffalo, Tarik opened the hatch to a cellar. He had to duck to go down the stone steps; he reached to screw in a bulb dangling from a beam. Metal-grated windows, two-feet-by-one-foot, lined the underground room. The concrete floor was scuffed to dirt in patches. The air was musty. He walked to another dangling lightbulb and screwed it in. Below it was a rusted metal kitchen table—a Coca-Cola insignia worn thin in the center—a stool with a ripped black vinyl seat, and a mattress that he had pulled from a Dumpster. On the table sat a radio/cassette player with wire dangling from the antenna's broken tip and a cassette tape, a Koran covered in plastic wrap, a gallon jug of water, a packet of sewing needles and a spool of thread, scissors, a chisel, and a bench knife. Next to the knife Tarik had started the pharmaceutical section, with the bennies and everything else he had stolen from a drugstore: hydrogen peroxide, nail polish remover, and small brown apothecary glass bottles of ammonia nitrate and aluminum powder. Arranged at one end was more stuff he had been gathering since his return: white nylon the size of a torso that he had already sewn together on three sides; several hollowed-out rectangular wood strips and pieces of cotton cloth to fit inside them, a quart of carpenter's glue, jars of ball bearings, tiny brown hardware-store bags—like the ones penny candy used to come in—filled with nails, screws, bolts, nuts. In a Dunkin' Donuts cup were pieces of a penlight—bulb, switch, battery—and a couple of thin wires. Finally, standing upright were five-inch lengths of plumbing pipes surrounded by a bunch of metal caps.

Tarik poured a glass of water and fished out a pill, just one because he wanted to concentrate; he wanted to see whether he could sleep later. He had considered driving a Checker, volunteering to prowl the worst East Side neighborhoods, but the job would have required a background check, fingerprints. He had been told in the desert that he would be placed on the FBI list when he got home. Many *jihad* fighters landed on that list, but if he were careful nothing would happen to him. Allah had led him to Bakir, the black guy who owned the Bubble Brush—a Muslim ex-con, who liked the way Tarik spoke Arabic and recited from the Koran. The guy called him "brother," paid him for power-washing the Lincolns and Mustangs of pimps and pushers, and let him squat in the cellar until he could get back on his feet. Tarik had lied and told Bakir he had been in Attica for knocking off drugstores to satisfy his craving for whiz. The guy was a dope, no more on the path that Allah had marked out than any of the Yemenis who would rather play soccer than search for paradise. He thought, *I bet the bastard fucked a lot in prison. I've seen him look at me. One wrong move and I'll blow the faggot's ass right out a window.*

There was so much to do. He put in the cassette, lay on the mattress, and listened to what he had heard a hundred times before. He thought, *I've sewn the vest, tonight I'll assemble the shrapnel plates, and when the day comes, I'll mix the explosives and attach the detonator. But tonight the focus is shrapnel. Allahu akbar.* He replayed the instructions for laying the cotton cloth in the hollowed-out wood, arranging ball bearings into rows on the cotton so that it would look a little like a section cut out of a beehive, pouring the glue lightly over the steel balls and waiting the night for them to dry hard and fast into a deadly sheet.

He remembered suddenly the thin spool of wire he needed to weave strings of screws and nuts and bolts and nails, and smacked his forehead, hard, with his fist. He rewound the cassette to the ball bearings instructions, and stood. He wished there was a mirror in the cellar. He wished he had a holster and gun, a .44 tucked in the seat of his pants, a .38 in a holster under his arm. He would stand before the mirror like Travis Bickle. He would draw the .38, fast, again and again. He would reach back for the magnum and slide it around and hold it at arm's length, and fire—a make-pretend-fire, *pow*. He would hold his thumb and finger to his temple and whisper, *pow*. He thought, *Concentrate. Don't eat, don't sleep, don't shit.*

Days not weeks, soon hours not days, then minutes not hours, then seconds until . . . pow.

He thought about popping another bennie, but he shook his head and sat on the torn stool cushion. He rewound the cassette to the start of the shrapnel lesson even though he could recite each step, word for word. He knew it better than the Koran. He put his palms flat on the table and tried to imagine seventy-two virgins. He thought, *I'll show the imam he should have trusted me. I'm not a loser.* He wished he were in Palestine because there he would not need to do everything himself. There would be the Agent to select the target; the Engineer to prepare the bomb and its components; the Mule to take him close; the Planner to command the operation and know where he would have to stand or sit for the maximum kill. But here in the cellar he was alone, doing Allah's will.

Allahu Akbar, he said.

He was sorry there wasn't enough time to finish his vest for the *Maid of the Mist. Too bad,* he thought. *Allah's will.* But he was glad he had terrified Asim. *Father like son, both faggots, abomination, scum, easy to scare. I tried to help; now he can die.* He had seen his brother with the redhead queer in South Park. He had hidden inside the edge of the evergreen patch and heard everything, the FBI man too. He thought, *I'm tired of the filth and scum. I'm tired of America.*

He unscrewed the bulbs and lay on the mattress, knowing he wouldn't sleep.

Tuesday, September 11, 2001
TOWERING INFERNO

DID YOU HEAR THE thunderstorms last night?" Masika asked, placing a carton of milk on the table.

Sonia was watching the way her fingers had started curling inward. They hurt.

"So you didn't hear the thunderclaps?"

"Boom," Sonia said. In her head she started to sing "Stormy Weather."

"That's right, sonic ones."

"Your father hated the movie."

"What movie?"

"*Days of Thunder*, with that pretty boy Tim Cruise."

"Tom, honey."

Sonia ignored her. "Who wants to waste time watching cars crack up? But I said, 'Badru, I bet you wouldn't kick him out of bed.'"

"Here, eat some Cheerios," Masika said, shaking her head. She poured the cereal and milk into a bowl for Sonia. Eight-thirty and Asim was still in bed.

On the kitchen television, a talk show host Sonia didn't like was chatting with a man, who used to be obese until a doctor suctioned fat out of his stomach. Sonia couldn't remember the names of anyone on TV.

"He's jolly, even without the belly," she said.

The woman was smiling like a high school cheerleader and said from a feed inside the studio: "It's just the most beautiful September Tuesday in New York City." The host reminded Sonia of the girls Sandra Dee used to hang out with in those bad beach movies. She never liked Gidget.

She told Masika, "That woman stinks."

"You think so? She's popular."

Outside, in Rockefeller Plaza, tourists had surrounded the guy with the mike and applauded the woman when they heard her say, "New York City."

Someone else chimed in. "Okay, tell me, who are all those good-looking ladies in uniform?" The camera panned across the dozen policewomen, who were screaming, "We love New York!"

"These are the cops of the month, from the Women Police Officers of America Association, and their calendar is hot."

One of the cops was leaning in to talk about raising money for domestic abuse victims, when the host interrupted and the shot shifted to flames shooting out of a skyscraper:

"We have some breaking news to go to. There's a fire at the World Trade Center."

The television showed an immense plume of smoke rising from one of the buildings, while the host and another voice speculated there had been an explosion. Someone else broke in and said it appeared that a plane had crashed into the tower, a private jet perhaps, while someone else said he didn't think a small plane, like a Piper, could cause so much dense smoke. There was a jumble of television voices talking over the images of the fire. A different angle on the building appeared: explosive flames shot from what looked like a volcanic gash.

The host said a witness saw a jet with the insignia AA on the tail. Someone wondered whether it was a hijacking, and the host said it was foolish to speculate. Someone else said commercial airliners don't fly anywhere near the towers.

There was a quick shot of the crowd inside the TV station plaza: tourists in baseball caps and T-shirts with their eyes fixed on the huge outdoor television screen, the calendar cops—stunned and silent, the metal sculpture of Atlas holding up Earth in the background.

Sonia was mesmerized when one of the television chatterers said that the scene at the towers looked like a movie. She fixed her attention on the grandeur of the calamity, and thought, *It looks like* The Towering Inferno.

Someone said the city's 9-1-1 emergency system was over-loaded. The host said the first fire companies were on the scene and the two towers were ordered evacuated. Someone broke in and said the police chief had declared the highest level of emergency and police from all over the city were rushing to Lower Manhattan. The guy in the plaza said, "It's unbelievable, it's like the movie *The Towering Inferno.*"

Sonia thought, *Amazing, he thinks like me.*

Her eyes remained fixed on the small television at the end of the table. The explosive flames had disappeared, and smoke shot sky-ward revealing the gash where the plane had crashed through the building; the tear was floors wide. The smoke turned gray and thick as it engulfed the patch of blue sky between the towers.

"Asim," Masika yelled. "Get down here." She stood beside Sonia, an arm resting on the old woman's shoulder.

Sonia remembered in *The Towering Inferno* there was no way down, no way out. She thought, *The cast was epic. Who wasn't in it? Even the old Buffalo Bill who got away with murder.*

"Who was the football player who killed his wife and her lover?" she asked.

Masika ignored her.

"He was in *The Towering Inferno.* "

Maskika gave her a look and said, "O.J. Simpson."

"That's the guy. He couldn't act."

Someone on the television said something about the 1993 World Trade Center bombing and someone else said it was imprudent to suggest a link to terrorism—it could have been a terrible accident.

Masika whispered, "God help us."

"What does God have to do about anything? A disaster is a disaster, you should know this." Sonia said. "You think God cares about a burning building?"

Asim appeared in shorts and a white T-shirt. Sonia thought, *He's really a beautiful boy.*

"What's going on?" he asked.

It was 9:03. Sonia said, "It's like a movie."

"A plane crashed into the World Trade Center. It's burning," Masika said.

"Look," Asim said.

The three watched another jet arc toward the corner of the second tower and slam into it: the burst of mountainous flames and smoke, a rain of shattering glass that gleamed in the sunshine. Voices on the television returning to a single refrain, something like *Oh my God, another plane.* Then, for many seconds, no one on the television or in the kitchen said a word.

Sonia finally said, "What's happening?"

Someone on the television said, "Two passenger jets crashing into the buildings can't be an accident."

Smoke from the second tower swelled like the trough of an enormous black wave. Asim switched channels—ABC, CBS, CNN, Fox—each with the same shot of the burning and smoking towers. Someone said that Boston's Logan Airport had cancelled all scheduled takeoffs, and it appeared the first jet that crashed into the North Tower was an American Airlines flight from Boston. "Unbelievable," a voice off camera said. Someone wondered whether the president had been informed.

"My God," someone said. "I think there are people standing at the windows. My God, they're jumping."

Sonia thought she saw a body falling and pointed, "There's one."

Again a reporter mentioned the 1993 bombing.

Masika looked at Asim. "Do you think Tarik's involved?"

He didn't answer.

Meanwhile, the screen was filled with the burning tower and in the top right corner was the rerun of the airliner curving and slamming into it. Someone said there was an order to halt air traffic nationwide. Mayor Giuliani had ordered City Hall, the United Nations, and the Empire State Building evacuated.

"Lucy's father is going to think he's involved," Asim said.

"Call the FBI," Masika said.

Sonia said, "Your father used to say, 'watch your back around Tarik.'"

Asim said: "What am I going to say? 'You were right. He's the kind of brother who blows things up?'"

Everyone was silent and watched the flames and smoke on the television.

Finally, Asim said, "He's crazy enough. But an airliner? Anyway, he couldn't be on a plane, because he's in town."

"He could have left yesterday," Masika said.

"I guess so. He didn't show up at the *Maid of the Mist*."

"What are you talking about?"

"I didn't tell you. I was supposed to meet him in Niagara Falls. I wanted to handle it."

"Handle what?" she asked.

He didn't answer.

"You were supposed to meet him on the boat and he didn't show up. Maybe he did leave town. Maybe he was on one of the planes."

Asim looked at the television.

"Call the FBI," she repeated.

The newscasts looped over and over the footage of the burning North Tower while the second jet, a United flight from Boston, slammed into the South Tower. President Bush, outside a school in Florida, appeared live in the corner of the screen. Huddled around him were Secret Service agents who looked in a hurry to whisk him away.

They listened to the president, who was finishing a statement:

"Terrorism against our nation will not stand. And now if you would join me in a moment of silence. May God bless the victims, their families, and America. Thank you very much."

Sonia said, "What's he thanking us for? I don't understand."

Masika looked at her brother and shook her head. He said he'd go upstairs and call Lucy's father.

Sonia asked, "Did you see *Fail-Safe?*

Masika ignored her.

A few minutes later, Asim returned and said, "He'll be here before noon. He wants to talk to everyone."

It was 9:53. Someone broke in and said, "The Pentagon has been attacked."

"It keeps getting worse," Masika said with a little moan.

Asim wasn't listening, and said, "He wasn't always crazy. He used to laugh. Can you remember what made him happy?"

Three was a knock on the door, which Masika answered. When she returned Billy was with her.

Sonia said, "Did anyone ever tell you, you look a little like Gary Cooper?"

Billy didn't answer.

"A plane just hit the Pentagon," Asim said.

"I heard it on the radio."

Sonia looked back at the burning towers and thought of what Nicky had said about flames that shot from stacks at the Bethlehem Steel Mill: "Like generations burning," he had told her. She was crying softly. *Poor Nicky,* she thought. *I should have helped him. If he knew how miserable I'd be, maybe he wouldn't have jumped into the furnace.*

Billy leaned in and whispered, "You okay, Sonia?"

Asim turned away from the television and watched Billy take her hand and rest it on his.

It was 9:59. Masika whispered, "My God, the tower is collapsing."

CHALKY STRANGERS

TARIK WOKE UP and coughed. He could taste dirt in his mouth. His nose and lungs were filled with must. He looked at his watch, surprised that it was 9:45. He had slept almost four hours, more sleep than in hundreds of nights. He sat up and stretched, shifted free of the spring poking him, and looked at the table. It was almost finished. All he needed to do was mix the powder in the pipes, cap them, and sew shut the top of the vest. He had about eighty dollars—enough for a room at the Iron Ore Inn in Lackawanna and whatever else he needed. But he thought, *Bakir will give me a hundred, if I ask. I can stay at the Buffalo Statler, order room service, wash myself in a marble tub, shave, buy appropriate*

clothes. After weeks in this cellar, I could use a good ablution. Allah says
martyrs are blessed.

He put a hand flat on the dirt floor to help himself up. His hip
ached from sleeping on his side, which the *Tablighi Jamaat* required. He put on pants—filthy mahogany Dickies—and led with
his right leg, according to the teachings. There were so many habits
of the Prophet Mohammad that he could not emulate because he
had to be careful not to arouse suspicion, but he understood his
sacrifices would be rewarded. He was glad he could shave his upper lip, but dared not let his beard grow. He let the pants cuffs fall
below his ankles even though he knew that the prophet said allow-
ing clothes to drag was a sign of arrogance. He picked up the bottle of bennies and fished out one with his index finger and thumb,
the way one must eat according to the *Tablighi Jamaat,* and placed
the pill on his tongue. He poured a glass of water and said, *"Allahu*
akbar." The prophet would understand that a warrior does whatever he must. It is *jihad* that matters. The warrior had to remain at-
tentive, and if a white pill helped, the prophet wouldn't condemn
him. Even Shamal, who had turned into an enormous disappointment, was right when he had told the stupid Yemeni boys that they
were visitors in America, travelers far from their Muslim roots. In
a foreign land, a visitor can indulge.

He knew he had indulgences, but he was more serious than most
everyone. He had chiseled in the concrete cellar wall a faint row of
clock faces showing the times of Islam's five daily prayers. Since
his return he was careful not to go near a mosque; in his basement
cave outside the car wash he kept his own *adhan.*

He thought of what Travis Bickle wrote in his diary: "I don't believe that one should devote his life to morbid self-attention." He wished that the imam had understood he was destined for sacrifice. He could be trusted. He could become a martyr. He could find purity. Tarik understood he was no one in this world, an isolated servant, and understanding his essential nothingness set him free to do God's will. *Who needs the imam?* he thought. *A warrior for Allah needs no approval. I'll show everyone I can do God's work. My life is in Allah's hands.*

He walked out of the cellar hatch to the car wash. Bakir was in the office, watching television.

Tarik said, "I want to take the day off, Bakir. Can you give me a hundred dollars? I have something important to do."

"Do you know what's happened? Watch this, Tarik. The World Trade Center has been destroyed."

Tarik watched the North Tower collapsing into a cloud of dust.

"They think our brothers did this. If it's true, I want to vo-vo-vo-vomit," Bakir said.

A guy in a Town Car had been honking at the bay of the car wash for a couple of minutes. The door was shut.

"Don't answer that asshole," Bakir said. "Why the fuck does he wa-wa-wa-want a car wash, with all that's happening?"

The clips of the collapsing towers stunned Tarik, and he thought, *This is it, the rumors of great things to come? And Shamal sent me home alone.* He had only this one clear thought: *I've been left out.*

Bakir said, "The bro-bro-bro-thers have gone too far." He picked up a string of wooden prayer beads from his desk and fidgeted with it. He mumbled something incomprehensible.

Tarik was confused. The bennies and his sleeplessness and the exploding towers were driving him now. His anger mounted. He looked at Bakir, as if this idiot had somehow become an obstacle in his path; the stuttering weakling sickened him. He fastened his arm around Bakir's neck and took out of his pocket the bench knife he had used to carve the trough into shrapnel molds and pressed the tip against Bakir's neck, covering the terrified man's mouth with his free hand and said, "If you scream, I'll cut your throat."

He turned to the television and saw a rerun of the first airliner crashing into the tower. He remembered the imam walking away from him in the desert as if he were someone easily discarded. In a voice that sounded in his skull far away, he said, "I am in Allah's hands," and as if he were outside his body watching himself, he was surprised by how easy it was to slit Bakir's throat from one ear to the other.

Tarik threw him down, and he landed face up, his eyes staring at nothing in particular. *The look of a man who had disappointed Allah,* Tarik thought.

He turned back to the television: men and women covered in concrete dust were running down streets away from the collapse. He looked at his blood-soaked T-shirt, then at Bakir's body, and thought, *Allah lets everything happen for a reason.*

He knew what drawer the money was in and bunched the bills into his pants pocket. He sat and looked at blood pooling at Bakir's shoulders; he ignored another horn blaring at the car wash bay. He watched the television and was sorry he was not a part of this great sacrifice. He was spellbound by jets slamming into skyscrapers, skyscrapers crumbling into dust, chalky strangers running everywhere.

QUE SERA SERA

I **T WAS SIX O'CLOCK** and Sonia lay awake in bed. She imagined being on the cot in the upstairs room of the Bethlehem and decided it was time to see Nicky and Badru. She didn't understand what was happening in New York; she didn't know what Tarik was up to. She was sick of this world. She had been listening to songs that Asim had "burned." She didn't know why the boy said he burned them. The CD didn't look damaged. Didn't he know she was tired of things burning?

She had just heard "Supercalifragilisticexpialidocious." She liked Julie Andrews and Dick Van Dyke and wondered why Asim had forgotten the song from *Victor/Victoria*. Didn't Asim know his father had adored it? The boy didn't know the half of it. She took out the earphone; the song was "Let's Call the Whole Thing Off," which she never liked. She didn't know what people saw in Fred Astaire. She pretended she was Julie Andrews dressed like a man anyone would die for, and sang, "*You and me . . . We're the kind of people other people would like to be . . . And we don't care that tomorrow comes with no guarantee . . . And care what you may . . . you and me . . . we'll stay together year after year.*"

Asim appeared at the door. "What's that song?" he asked.

"Your father loved it." She paused, and said, "From *Victor/Victoria.*"

"I never heard him sing it," he said.

"He kept secrets. Who doesn't?"

"Masika will be back in an hour. I'm meeting Billy at the basilica for a candlelight vigil."

"What about the FBI? I want to talk to them. I want to tell them everything I know."

"You don't know anything."

"I know Tarik's no good."

"They already know that. They're watching the house in case he shows up."

She had lost interest, and said, "I'm tired."

"Father would have been ashamed," he said.

"What do you know? He got tired, too."

"I mean about the attacks."

"What attacks?"

"You don't remember the towers?"

"I remember. I'm tired of fire."

He walked to the bed and asked, "You're okay, right?"

"Who's ever okay?"

He sat on the side of the bed, and said, "I wanted to close tonight, but Tony said it's bad luck to break a movie run. He's superstitious. Besides, he doesn't like crowds and isn't going to the vigil and doesn't want to stay home. He plays the movie even when no one shows up."

"The show must go on." She had come back enough to understand the theater would be open tonight. She was relieved. *I'm tired of this world,* she thought. *There's no better place to leave it than in the movie house.*

"I'll check in later, when I get back." He left.

She put the earphones back on and listened. It was Doris Day. She was singing "Que Sera, Sera."

TUXEDO JACKET

TARIK SCRUBBED the blood that had soaked through his T-shirt, and he thought, *I am a warrior for Allah*. The tub was a Jacuzzi, and he loved the way the jets massaged the soles of his feet. He stepped out and wrapped a towel around his neck. All of the walls of the bathroom were mirrored, and he didn't care whether he saw himself naked. Allah would forgive his indulgences.

In the closet he found a white terrycloth robe. He got the menu from the desk and picked out his dinner: For an appetizer he would have escargots. *Something French, for the occasion,* he thought. He ordered a wedge of iceberg lettuce covered with chopped walnuts, apples and chunks of blue cheese; surf and turf with lemon-and-oil asparagus and capers; a split of Moet; tiramisu; coffee and cognac. He fished out another bennie and washed it down with Perrier.

He took out clothes for his martyrdom. He wished he could wear a white robe like Mohammed, but instead leading with his right foot, he put on baggy black linen pants, no underwear. In a show of his humility, he didn't care if anyone noticed that he had rolled the cuffs a quarter of the way up his calves so that they wouldn't drag. He felt confident—in Allah's hands. He carefully picked up the vest and threaded an arm through one side and then the other. He pulled the three Velcro straps across his chest and fastened them, first the top, then the center, and finally the one that went across his waist. The vest felt sexy against his skin. *Why shouldn't it? I am a warrior.* He slipped on a silken white shirt, oversized too, so that it would fall inches above his knees. He put on a jacket, a formal dinner jacket, the kind with a satin stripe down the lapels, a tuxedo jacket for a wedding. It didn't cover the end of the shirt. He looked in the mirror. *The heft of the vest,* he thought, made him look handsome. He had already shaved his head. He sat to put on shiny black shoes from Payless. No socks. He was angry with himself that he had forgotten socks. He wished he could have worn sandals, but he thought, *The rolled-up pants are risky enough.*

There was a knock on the door: a young man with blond hair and a smile that pleased Tarik.

"Your dinner, sir," he said, wheeling the cart to the wing chair across from the television.

Tarik reached in his wallet, picked out a ten, and handed it to the waiter. *Twenty left. Enough for the cab,* he thought. "Your politeness is appreciated," he said.

The young man was surprised and nodded before he left.

Tarik turned on the television. The meal dulled the buzz of the speed, and while he watched the news, he regretted again that he was not a part of the spectacle; he wondered whether in the desert he had met any of the airplane warriors who were waiting for Allah's reward. He thought Shamal wouldn't be among them. *He's a coward and a hypocrite. I'll show him I am a worthy warrior.* On the television someone was interviewing a woman who was looking for her son, a waiter at Windows on the World. She held up a photograph and the camera zoomed in: a handsome face, dark eyes, and a pensive expression. His name was Antonio. She was crying. Tarik thought, *He looks like the kind of person who thinks "towelhead" when he sees an Arab.* He made a gun with his thumb and finger, pointed to the screen, and said, "pow." He clicked to another channel and watched the loop of the airliners slamming into the two towers, the buildings collapsing, lost men and women covered in concrete powder, wandering through lower Manhattan—a city haunted by walking statues.

He popped another pill and washed it down with the champagne. He thought, *Wait until they see what I can do.*

THE FAR DOOR

SONIA STEPPED OFF the bus at the Bethlehem. She was glad it was Tuesday and Johnny wasn't driving. She hadn't the time for makeup and still wore the housedress she had put on that morning. She was glad the bus was empty and no one except the strange driver saw what a mess her body had turned into. She was glad Asim wouldn't be there.

The lights of the marquee were flashing and the H from the feature had fallen off so that it read: FROM ELL. The driver said, "That's a stupid name for a movie. Anyway, I'm surprised it's open tonight."

She didn't say anything. She heard the bus engine boom as it pulled away and noted that the driver didn't wait for her to enter the lobby.

One by one she tried the doors, but was so confused she didn't think it was odd that only the far door was open. It was 7:10 and the movie had already begun. There was no one at the counter to sell her a ticket, so she walked to the center aisle, where, on the screen, she saw Johnny Depp on a couch in a dusky opium den.

She tried hard to remain as quiet as she could be when she climbed the stairs. Her legs trembled at each step, but she could tell she was going to make it. She felt stronger than she had been all week. Her hands on the rail barely shook. She wished she had remembered the Walkman. She would have liked to hear "As Time Goes By" and skip to "When You Wish upon a Star." Before she slept, she would have liked to hear, "The Man That Got Away." She would miss the songs. She wished Asim hadn't removed the *Sabrina* poster from the room. She thought, *Love is all that matters, and when it's gone, it's gone forever.* She stopped halfway up the steps and worried she had forgotten the pills. She felt the outside of her jacket for the bottle. Her pills were there. She needed all of them.

EVERYTHING'S PERSONAL

THE DOORMAN OUTSIDE the Statler hailed a cab for Tarik. He remembered he had only the twenty and said, "I'll catch you when I get back."

Tarik thought he'd caught the man sneering. But he decided to ignore it.

"Take me to Our Lady of Victory Basilica," he told the cab driver. The composure he felt in his hotel room had started to wane.

"The vigil?" the taxi guy asked. He was a kid really, black, with a sing-song Haitian voice.

"That's right, the vigil."

"Terrible thing," the kid said. "I couldn't believe it."

Tarik was silent.

The kid paused and asked, "Are you Arab?"

Tarik said, "It's a noble profession."

"What?"

"Taxi driver."

"Noble? My mother said I'm going to get killed someday if I don't give it up and go to school."

"Don't listen to her. We're all going to get killed," he said.

The kid didn't say anything.

Tarik picked a bennie out of his pocket and swallowed it, and asked, "Do you have any water?"

"Nope, but I can stop."

"Keep going."

"I heard people are packing into the basilica," the kid said.

He talked about the attacks, but Tarik had stopped listening. They had already reached the Skyway; Lake Erie looked otherworldly beyond the ruined mills and railroad yards. The sun at dusk was orange and swollen.

The kid said, "The sky's freaky."

Tarik could see the dome of Our Lady of Victory emerging at the end of the shore road; as they passed South Park the cab inched along in the traffic and the kid said, "Maybe you want to get out here. It will take me a while to drive to the front of the basilica."

"I'll wait," Tarik said.

"It's your money."

Tarik watched people streaming to the church steps, even Arab men from the neighborhood who walked hand in hand. He thought they should be home, thanking Allah for the martyrs' sacrifice.

Didn't they understand *jihad*? There were Christians, only a few Jews. He thought, *The best thing about Lackawanna is there are so few Jews.* They carried candles stuck into the bottom of Dixie cups. A few held photographs of the World Trade Center. He thought he saw Asim walking beside the Irish faggot in a crowd of priests from Father Baker's. He started to breathe heavily and felt faint. He sensed that if he popped another bennie, he might die. He didn't know why this was happening now while he was filled, finally, with a purpose that would please Allah; he felt abandoned by everything that was important to him. He had to escape the square and mumbled something the taxi driver didn't understand.

"You okay?" the kid asked.

"Turn, and get out of here," Tarik managed to say. "Take me to Abbott Road. There's a theater there called the Bethlehem."

"You sure."

"Just drive," he ordered.

"What's the matter?"

Tarik didn't answer and the kid didn't say another word until they got to the Bethlehem.

He had the twenty in his hand when the kid said, "That's fifteen bucks."

He handed over the bill and said, "You're lucky."

"Lucky. How?"

"You'll see."

As soon as Tarik got out, the kid drove off.

He was so high on pills and champagne that he didn't know what to think about anything. He didn't understand why he had fled from the square and felt even fainter, and worried that his weakness had angered Allah. He looked at the marquee and the letters swirled—ATRELFEE. The street was empty. All he could see was the cab, blocks away, turning left on its way back to Buffalo. He tried the middle lobby door but it was locked. He hoped the Russian bitch was inside. No matter how hard he tried to see things through Allah's teachings he feared that everything he did had become personal. *I'm still a warrior, I'll be forgiven indulgences,* he thought. He tried the next door—locked too—and the last one on the right, which opened into the lobby. Everything blurred. The chandeliers reminded him of shattering glass. He leaned against a wall and rested. He saw Shamal laughing as he pictured himself missing the targets with the Kalashnikov. *Scum,* he thought. *The imam will see I'm not scum.*

He passed through the outer lobby and heard the movie playing. He checked the office, even though he knew Asim and the redhead faggot were holding candles at the basilica. He figured Masika was at the hospital. But maybe the Russian bitch was inside, he thought. He could only hope. He pictured exploding in his father's chair, and decided it would be better in a red velvet movie seat, a better place to find peace, to pray, to honor Allah. He thought he heard someone move in the room upstairs—his father's fucking room. *It's the projectionist,* he decided. *Tony deserves to die as much as anyone. He used to look at me like he thought I was scum. Why shouldn't he pay? Why shouldn't everyone pay? I hope the old bitch is in her seat.* He walked down the center aisle and felt like laughing. He stopped to watch the screen. It was night on a street in another century. Gas lamps barely illuminated the scene. A horse and carriage halted, its door opened, the clap of the buggy's metal steps released. He watched Jack the Ripper climb out and thought his head was exploding. When Tarik reached the middle of the theater, he felt for the first seat, and sat down. He looked around for Sonia, but it was too dark to see. *This is Allah's will,* he thought. For a moment he didn't think about anything and then he said, loud enough so that others, if there had been anyone else inside, would have heard him: "Allah will not tolerate *abominations.*" He fished out his last bennie and popped it in his mouth. He knew he would keep his consciousness long enough to open his jacket, reach into his shirt, and pull the switch. Just before he detonated, Tarik had time to think: *I hate the world, and the world doesn't even notice me.*

AMAZING GRACE

A CRESCENT MOON floated over the dome of Our Lady of Victory, and from speakers across the basilica's porticos came voices of a boys' choir. A woman in a black dot dress held a poster of the Brooklyn Bridge, with the World Trade Center looming behind it. Asim pictured the towers aflame while the choir started to sing "Amazing Grace."

He had tried to honor the dead, but he couldn't keep his concentration on the vigil, even though hundreds of people carried votive candles and sang about the grace that they hoped would guide them through so much grief. Asim was ashamed, because even though he shared their anguish, he knew that later, when he left the

square, at just nineteen, he would be left with his own private bur-
den of a broken life: an old woman consumed by shaking, a brother
with a Kalashnikov strapped across his back, a boyfriend he was
afraid to love. Sonia was right. The day had played out a little like
a movie. He pictured her with his father, night after night, side by
side in the Bethlehem. Didn't they see that when a movie ended,
they were alone with the same lives they had left when the lights
had gone out? Even the spectacular burning towers, which had
captivated everyone that morning like some celluloid explosion,
couldn't keep Asim from feeling sorry for himself. He stopped
thinking and tried to listen to "Amazing Grace." He noticed Billy,
deep in a prayer, and thought, *Why can't I be as good a man?*

The first blast came from the direction of the Bethlehem and
sounded like a truck backfiring. A priest next to him looked up. The
second blast boomed and the choir stopped. Some people, visibly
nervous, started to leave the basilica square. In the distance, smoke
plumes drifted across the sky. A fire siren blared.

Asim took Billy's hand. "What do you think happened over
there?"

Billy didn't know. "Maybe we should go see."

He shook his head and leaned into his boyfriend. Why should
Asim care whether anyone noticed how much he wanted to love?
He closed his eyes and listened for what else might shatter the sky.

ACKNOWLEDGMENTS

Without the encouragement of friends, I would probably be a very different writer. I'm grateful to Barbara and Sheldon Fried, Sarah Shepard and Garth Green, Rita Rogers and Charles Duncan, Sylvia and Fritz Lahvis, and Wendy Barry for their friendship. I thank my sister-in-law, Peggy Zebrun, who grew up in Lackawanna around the corner from Our Lady of Victory Basilica, for sharing memories about Father Nelson Baker's Home for Boys and her steel town. I'm grateful for the childhood memories that the movies and people at the Abbott Theater in Lackawanna have given me.

This novel has had many helpful readers, including Joseph Pittman and Greg Herren. An enormous thanks to my editor, Sarah Van Arsdale, for her close editorial eye and enthusiasm. The support and advice of my agent, Michael Bourret, has been invaluable. And, about my greatest thanks, it's hard to imagine this novel existing without the friendship and editorial help of Jim and Karen Shepard.